YOUNG
AND
INNOCENT

A NOVEL BY

EDWIN
WEST

BLACKBIRD BOOKS
NEW YORK • LOS ANGELES

A Blackbird Classic, September 2011

Copyright © 1960 by Edwin West

Cover painting by Robert Maguire

Manufactured in the United States of America.

The events and characters depicted in this book are fictional.

Cataloging-in-Publication Data

West, Edwin.
Young and innocent / Edwin West.
p. cm.
1. Lesbians—Fiction. 2. Publishers and publishing—Fiction.
3. Woman executives—Sexual behavior—Fiction. 4. Trian-
gles (Interpersonal relations)—Fiction. 5. I. Title.
PS3573.E9 Y6 2011 813′.54—dc22 2011937787

Blackbird Books
www.bbirdbooks.com
email us at editor@bbirdbooks.com

ISBN 978-1-61053-003-3

First Blackbird Edition

10 9 8 7 6 5 4 3 2 1

YOUNG
AND
INNOCENT

1

THE ELEVATOR doors slid back and Lavinia Cartwright, breathing fire, clacked high heels through the steno pool. The furious chatter of typing, which had started thirty seconds before Lavinia's entrance, continued until thirty seconds after her exit through the green door to Editorland, then grew ragged and arrhythmic and faltered to silence.

Steno One: "She's boiling this morning."

Steno Two: "Look out for falling axes."

Steno Three: "Thank God I'm getting married. No more—"

The green door flashed open and Lavinia's face reappeared. "Are you people paid to type or talk?"

Nine typewriters shifted into high gear. The green door slammed. The typing didn't slow down.

The girls in the steno pool could set their watches by Lavinia Cartwright. Every morning, without fail, she was twenty minutes late for work. Since she was editor-in-chief of *Milady* ("The Modern Monthly for Modern Women"), this was her privilege. Since she had been editor-in-chief for eight years, this was a privilege-become-habit.

Now, at forty, Lavinia looked both older and younger than her actual age. Her face was older, a strong and sharp and predatory face, not "good-looking" by any calendar girl standard, but unusually attractive in an aggressive and harsh-lined and totally individual way. Her body looked younger than forty, slim-waisted, high-breasted, firm-hipped, with strong shoulders and slender legs. It cost quite a bit to keep the body so young. Money for daily massage and heat-lamp treatments, for exercise equipment and a doctor-surveyed diet. Money for an annual month-long vacation on the western coast of Florida. The money was well spent, the body was barely thirty while the face was forty-five, and the birth certificate seemed hopelessly inaccurate when it claimed that Lavinia was forty.

Lavinia had become editor-in-chief of *Milady* eight years before, when she was thirty-two. Thirty-two was also the median age of the woman for which *Milady* was edited and at which *Milady* was aimed, and this had been one of Lavinia's strong selling points when she went after the job. No one had pointed out to her that her argument was self-defeating, that she should have been replaced on her thirty-third birthday by someone a year younger. The fact was that Lavinia loathed her readers just enough to understand them. She was the perfect editor for *Milady,* a magazine aimed, as she once said, "at married women with upper-class tastes and middle-class income."

Having goosed the steno pool into working, Lavinia now marched down the long hall flanked by afterthought partitions toward her office. Chalmers-Mead, publishers of *Milady* and seven other magazines, leased three floors in this Park Avenue building, eighteen through twenty. *Milady* being the firm's biggest, most important and most profitable magazine, it had the entire nineteenth floor to itself.

As Lavinia now stormed down the hall, she passed the IBM-whirring subscription department and the cubicles and sub-offices of all the editorial and administrative divisions; and the farther she moved from the elevator, the more important in the editorial hierarchy the people occupying the offices became. A strange reversal, but true.

At the very end of the hall stood a lone door, its frosted glass marked in gold with Lavinia's name. Above the name was the word "EDITOR"; below, "PRIVATE." Lavinia reached the door and stalked in.

Lavinia's personal secretary, Miss Henderson, was typing rapidly and effortlessly. Without pausing, she nodded at Lavinia. "Good morning, Miss Cartwright."

"Get me Sandra." Lavinia strode on through to her own office, hung up her coat, and sat behind her massive and well-littered desk.

The box beside her left hand buzzed and Lavinia depressed the left-hand switch. "Yes?"

"Miss Keel isn't in yet, Miss Cartwright."

"I want to see her the minute she arrives."

"Yes, Miss Cartwright."

Lavinia broke the connection and glowered at the mass of papers on her desk. "This time," she muttered, "you've gone too far."

No one could set a watch by Sandra Keel. Her arrival at work meant only that the time was somewhere between nine A.M. and noon. Whereas Lavinia was predictably late and lateness was her privilege, Sandra Keel was unpredictably late and had no right to be. The girls in the steno pool grumbled, behind Sandra's back, that she was the editor's pet. They had no idea how right they were.

Until seven months ago, Sandra Keel had been a free-lance commercial artist, making a fairly good living doing magazine and advertising illustrations. Seven months ago, Sandra and Lavinia met at a cocktail party. Within the week, Sandra was the new editorial assistant, Lavinia's vice-president. The editorial staff bitched about it, but only in whispers. They had all liked Mrs. Duffy, whom Sandra had replaced. It was difficult to like Sandra Keel. It was even more difficult to understand why Lavinia had hired her.

This morning, the second Monday in September, Sandra emerged from the elevator at fifteen minutes to ten. The steno pool was still working, and she walked on by without an exchange of greetings.

Sandra was twenty-eight, and looked it. Her figure was slender, her face oval, straight-nosed and high-boned, her ash-blond hair pulled straight back to a tight bun above the collar of a severely tailored gray suit. She was tall, and walked like a tall girl, with long straight strides.

Sandra's office was the last door on the right. She entered, and her secretary, Mrs. Marshall, looked up from her typing to say, "Miss Cartwright wants to see you right away, Miss Keel."

"She'll wait," said Sandra, "until I get my coat off. Silly bitch."

Mrs. Marshall had worked for five editorial assistants. She expected to work for the sixth as well, and possibly the seventh. She gave no answer to Sandra's comment.

Lavinia was pacing the broadloom before her desk when Sandra came in. She paced with her hands clasped behind her back, her head thrust forward, her lips thinned to a bloodless line, her eyes glaring at the wall.

"You wanted me?"

Lavinia stopped her pacing. "Shut the door."

Sandra half-smiled and closed the door. "You're mad at me," she said. "I can tell."

"Where were you last night?"

Sandra shrugged. "Out."

Lavinia made an angry gesture. "That isn't what I want to talk about. I want to talk about—" She circled her desk, rummaged through the papers atop it, came out with a letter on pale blue stationery. "About this," she said, and held the letter out for Sandra to take.

Sandra accepted the letter and glanced through it. It was from Miriam Staples Rider, a fiction writer who had often appeared in *Milady*, with short stories and novelettes and serials. The letter stated that *Never a Bridesmaid*, the four-part serial she had just completed, had been submitted to and accepted by *Woman's World*, *Milady's* chief competition. The letter further explained that this was due to the insulting correspondence from Miss Sandra Keel, in relation to *Many a Man*, Miss Rider's most recent serial in *Milady's* pages. The letter concluded with the hope that *Milady* could get along without Miriam Staples Rider as well as Miriam Staples Rider could get along without *Milady*.

Sandra dropped the letter back on Lavinia's desk. "Good riddance," she said calmly.

"Miriam is our top author," said Lavinia. Her face was tight, half-moons of bloodless white on either side of her mouth betraying the struggle she was having controlling herself. "We get more mail on her work than any other fiction writer we publish."

"We can get along without her," said Sandra. "Build somebody else up. Alice Clothier, maybe."

Sandra's calm served only to infuriate Lavinia even more. "How many letters did you write to Miriam?"

"I don't know, three or four."

"Without showing me a one of them."

"I don't show you every letter I send out."

"You should."

"Why?"

Lavinia clenched her fists. "Because I'm editor of this magazine, that's why. Because I spent years getting exclusive rights to Miriam's work, that's why. Because—what did you say in these letters?"

"There were some serious weaknesses in *Many a Man*. I pointed them out—you remember I talked to you about it when she sent it in—"

"And I disagreed with you."

"I merely pointed them out, suggested she be more careful in any more work she cared to submit to us. She wrote back a rather snotty letter—"

"Where were you last night?"

"I was out. Do you want to talk about—"

"Out where?"

"None of your business. Do you want to talk about this Rider thing or—"

"Where do you find the *gall*—how can you have the nerve to—"

"Oh, come on Lavinia, calm down. No one writer is that important, and you know it as well as I do."

"Miriam Staples Rider is a top name, a *selling* name—"

"So is Alice Clothier."

Lavinia sat down all at once and peered suspiciously across her desk at Sandra. "What's between you and Alice Clothier?"

"I don't even know the woman, I'm simply giving you an example—"

"She lives right here in New York."

"So do eight million other people. So what? If you're going to start getting jealous—"

"Where were you last night? You didn't come home at all."

"I went to a party, if you must know. It turned into an all-night affair and we all had breakfast together. But nothing happened, not a thing. Except I haven't had any sleep. And I come in here, first thing in the morning—"

"You had no *right* to antagonize Miriam."

"You gave me the job, Lavinia. Part of my job is correspondence with the authors. You never said I had to clear every letter through you."

"I never said you could push one of our authors over to *Woman's World* either."

"Just because I gave the woman some constructive criticism—"

"*You?* How much do you think you know—"

"Lavinia, you gave me the job, and the responsibility that goes with it."

"Maybe that was a mistake."

"Do you want to get rid of me? Say the word, Lavinia, and I'll move out today. Completely. Pack my things, go back to my old apartment—"

Lavinia shook her head wearily. "Stop being stupid, Sandra. You know I don't want you to leave me."

"Honey, it was a hell of a way to start the week. I come in here, and right off the bat—"

"You should have had more sense than to treat Miriam that way."

"I had no idea she was going to get on her high horse. She obviously didn't have any loyalty to *Milady,* to go running off to *Woman's World* over a little thing like that. And if she can't take constructive criticism—"

"Let me see the carbons of your letters. Maybe I can sweet-talk her—"

"There aren't any carbons. Mrs. Marshall didn't type these up, I did them myself, and I forgot to make carbons."

Lavinia studied the younger woman. "We make carbons of all correspondence," she said. "You know that as well as I do."

"It was just a letter pointing out one or two rough spots in Miss Rider's work—"

"There were four letters. You said so yourself. What about the other three?"

"She wrote back, a rather snotty letter—"

"Why didn't I see it?"

"It was addressed to me."

"I don't care who it was addressed to. Why didn't I see it? You know I should see every piece of mail that comes in from our top authors. Every piece."

"This had strictly to do with my letter, Lavinia, so I took it and answered it."

Lavinia searched the other woman's face, seeing only bland assurance and innocence there. She reached out to the intercom and buzzed for her secretary.

"Yes, Miss Cartwright?"

"Get me Miriam Rider's folder."

Sandra strolled across the room to the window overlooking Park Avenue. Down to the left was the back of Grand Central Station and the beginning of the avenue. Across the street, a new office building was going up. Nineteen floors down, cabs and occasional passenger cars rushed by on either side of the central green divider. "There's no need for all this fuss, you know," she said softly. "No need at all."

"I want to know what's going on behind my back."

"It isn't behind your back. It's the job you gave me. Don't give me responsibility and then complain when I accept it."

"This isn't accepting responsibility, Sandra. It's going behind my back, sabotaging a relationship with an author that took me years to build up."

"For heaven's sake, Lavinia," said Sandra, turning away from the window and coming back to the desk. "It's done. It happened, and there's nothing to be gained from arguing about it forever and ever."

"I don't want it to happen again."

"All right. It won't happen again. Every time I write a letter or approve an illustration or blow my nose, I'll run in here and ask you if it's all right."

"You know as well as I do that isn't what I mean. Approving an illustration is one thing. Antagonizing one of our top authors is something else again."

Sandra shook her head. "You're getting so touchy lately," she said. "When I first moved in with you, you were never like this. You used to be a wonderful person, Lavinia. I used to love being with you—everywhere, at the office, out at parties, at home, in bed—"

"Who was at this party last night?"

"Just some people—artists and so on. Nobody you know."

"Was Alice Clothier there?"

"I told you, I don't even know Alice Clothier. You've been getting more and more jealous lately."

"You've been staying out all night lately."

"I still have my own life to live, Lavinia." Sandra smiled and came around the desk to touch Lavinia's cheek gently with her fingertips. "Don't worry, honey, I'm not two-timing you."

"You're taking me for all you can get," said Lavinia.

"That's unkind, Lavinia. Unkind, and untrue. I haven't taken a thing from you. I pay half the rent, buy my own clothes, pay my own way all the time. I'm not taking anything from you."

"You're trying to take my magazine away from me."

"That's silly, and you know it. Lavinia, I'm sorry I stayed out last night. It won't happen again. That's what this fight is all about, isn't it?"

Lavinia nodded, reluctantly. "I suppose so."

"There's no need to be jealous, honey. There really isn't."

A light tap at the door caused Sandra to stop her stroking of Lavinia's cheek and move back around to the other side of the desk. Lavinia called, "Come in."

Miss Henderson, Lavinia's secretary, came in with a manila folder. "Miriam Rider's folder, Miss Cartwright," she said.

"Just leave it on the desk."

The folder was put on the desk, and both women stared at it, until the door closed again behind Miss Henderson. Then Sandra came back around the desk, saying, "Honey, don't be jealous of me, don't be so possessive."

"I can't help it," said Lavinia. "When you're out all night—"

"It won't happen again." Sandra leaned down and kissed Lavinia gently on the lips. "Am I forgiven?" she whispered.

Lavinia closed her eyes. The younger woman's breathing was so close, her slender figure so near . . . "Yes," she whispered. "It's all right, Sandra."

"Good." Sandra kissed her again, more forcefully this time, and straightened. "I'd better get back. I was supposed to have a meeting with the layout people at ten o'clock."

"All right," said Lavinia.

"I'll see you at lunchtime."

"Right."

Lavinia sat wearily behind her desk after Sandra had left. After a moment, she picked up the telephone, said, "Outside," and dialed a number. She waited, and when a woman's voice answered she said, "Alice? Lavinia Cartwright."

"Lavinia! How are you?"

"I'm fine. I was just wondering—Sandra and I happened to be talking about you—"

"Who?"

"Sandra. Sandra Keel."

"Oh, that's right, she's working for you now, isn't she?"

"She's been here for months. You know her, don't you?"

"Sandra? Of course. We went to the same school together. Different graduating classes, but same school. I was two years ahead of her."

"I see."

"She's a real worker, that girl. I remember, she was illustrator for the school paper, the year I was editor. Worked like a beaver."

"Yes, she does. At any rate, what I was calling about—we haven't seen anything from you in I don't know how long."

"I took a little vacation, Lavinia, as a matter of fact. Just got back Friday, and up till now it's been nothing but party, party, party. I'm hoping to be able to get down to work sometime this week."

"If you're thinking of doing a serial, in three or four parts, I'd love to see it first."

"You definitely will."

"Fine. Good to talk to you again."

"Good to hear from you, Lavinia. Bye now."

"Bye now."

Lavinia put the receiver back in its cradle and sat staring at it. Sandra had lied. Lied once, about knowing Alice Clothier.

Lied twice, about whom she'd been with last night. Lied who knew how many times, on how many subjects.

Why? Why did Sandra have to be like this, why did she have to lie and hide and sneak behind Lavinia's back? Why did she have to be so power-hungry with the magazine? That was the only reason she would have antagonized Miriam. Just to prove to herself that she could do it, and get away with it. And she could prove to herself that she could swing the buying over to the people *she* chose.

Why did it have to be that way? It had seemed, in the beginning, as though it would be so much better. The two of them, working together, living together, sharing interests and ideas and lives . . . In the beginning, it had been so different. . . .

Lavinia hadn't wanted to go to the party. She was a working editor, not a partying editor. She didn't have the personality for the role, she couldn't make inane small talk with inane people, she couldn't buy magazine rights to the next bestseller while sitting in somebody's crowded living room with a drink in her hand. Business was to be transacted behind a desk, and few in her field were better at it than Lavinia. But at the same time, few people were worse cocktail diplomats than Lavinia.

To make matters worse that afternoon, she had come with Greg, and Greg had ditched her. It was almost to be expected that he would. So many people present had more money than Lavinia, more power than Lavinia, more, in short, to offer Greg than did Lavinia. So she was alone, and Greg could be dimly seen through the cluster of conversationalists, over on the far side of the room with some stupid matron.

Charming, charming Greg. Where had she ever picked him up, anyway? Then all at once she remembered, the party given by Jake Stoneman when the new circulation figures had come out and *Milady* had surged ahead of *Today's Woman*. And there was Greg, brought by . . . by somebody, she wasn't sure who. Another Lavinia, she supposed now, to be ditched for someone better as Lavinia was now being ditched.

But oh, he had been so lovely. "What do you do?" The whimsical half-smile, the slight shrug, and, "Oh, I fool around with cameras. I'm a very bad photographer." The truth, told in such a way as to keep you from seeing it was the truth.

And, really, he hadn't picked her up at all. Well, of course he *had*, but so smoothly, so neatly, she had thought all along that she had picked him up. And that first evening, just coffee together in a tiny West Side luncheonette, that was all, and he'd insisted on paying for the cab and wouldn't come upstairs. "No, it's late and you're a working girl." Girl! Lavinia, what a fool you are, after all.

And the next meeting. By chance? It had seemed so, the accidental encounter on the sidewalk as Lavinia was leaving work. Dinner? Dinner. A night-cap? A night-cap. This was Friday, and the working girl could sleep late tomorrow.

Bed? Bed. And all at once he was living there, as though he had lived there always, and of course he shared expenses. Why not? He was now making better money, what with his assignments from *Milady*.

Stupid, stupid, stupid . . . How slowly, but how inexorably, the veneer had cracked, and the charming lover had become the petulant master. "Not tonight, Lavinia, I'm tired.

And I really don't see why I couldn't have been the one to go to Paris on that fashion spread." "I didn't want you to be away from me, Greg." "It was only three weeks." How to tell him that he didn't get the assignment because his work was too banal, too uninspired, that photos of fashionable living rooms were all he was capable of taking?

Turning away from her in the bed—punishing her—and grumbling, "I've never been to Paris."

And on those nights when he didn't turn his back, less and less frequently, how perfunctory he was! Rolling on top of her, face expressionless, hurrying to be done with it, rolling away at once, his back toward her, quickly asleep and leaving her staring, unsatisfied, at the ceiling.

Stupid, stupid . . . It was the bottom of a long and gradual slope, and Lavinia hadn't realized until tonight just how far down she had slid. Twenty years ago—no, fifteen, even ten years ago—the roles had been switched. Lavinia was young, her skin was fresh, she was attractive in a harsh and bitter way, and she could pick her men. And always the man she picked was someone who could do Lavinia Cartwright some good. *They* gave, *she* took.

When had the change taken place? At no one time, with no one man. It was a gradual change, an unnoticeable change. But the quality of her men grew poorer, and slowly the positions had been reversed, and her affairs were with young writers, illustrators, photographers, and *she* was the one who was giving—influence and backing and support— and *they* were the ones taking.

Not gigolos, not yet, not quite that far down the slope. But close, perilously close. And Greg was the bottom of the barrel, a so-so photographer living on assignments from

Milady and the other magazines in the Chalmers-Mead group.

And now even he was gone. And who would come after him, who could possibly come after him, but someone even worse?

For one of the few times in her life, Lavinia regretted the fact that she had never married. There had been one man— but they'd both been too young, then, they'd both been terrified of ties and personal responsibilities, and now it was far too late. Eighteen years too late.

She would live alone. Before she would sink to supporting some simpering gigolo, she would live alone, like it or not.

It was at that point that Sandra Keel sat down on the sofa beside her, saying, "Hi. What are you doing, sitting here all alone?"

Lavinia was used to seeing people quickly, seeing them whole, and judging them in one rapid surveyal. Looking up now, she saw a young girl in her late twenties, with a rather long and somewhat bony face, a touch of pale lipstick her only make-up. She had ash-blond hair, pulled back from her face and knotted in back. Her figure was good, but slender, almost thin. She was built like the girls who pose for fashion photographs, and Lavinia automatically assumed that this was what the girl did for a living. "That's right," she said, in answer to her question. "I'm sitting here all alone."

The girl immediately stood up again. "I'm sorry," she said. "If I'm intruding—"

Lavinia's own words came back to her, and she realized she'd been harsher than she'd intended. She'd been downright rude. She forced a smile and said. "No, that's all right. Really. Don't mind me. I'm just down in the dumps."

"I'll leave you alone, then," said the girl.

"No, please. I'd like to have someone to talk to, actually. If you wouldn't mind?"

"Not at all," said the girl, smiling, and she sat down again.

They exchanged names and surface information about one another, and Lavinia learned that her first guess had been wrong. Sandra Keel was a commercial artist. "You've done some things for us, haven't you? At *Milady*."

Sandra nodded, smiling again. "Just a couple. You pay awfully good money."

"Why haven't I met you?"

"I worked with Mrs. Duffy. Your assistant, isn't she?"

They talked, and they learned that both knew many of the same people, and so they discussed, inevitably, the oddness of fate, that people could share mutual friends for years and somehow never meet. When this subject ran down, they switched to magazines, from which both made their living, and moved on to the subject of art. Lavinia had an instinctive distaste for nonobjective art, and it turned out that Sandra shared the feeling.

Two hours had passed. It was impossible, but the party was breaking up, it was nine o'clock in the evening, and two hours had disappeared completely.

Lavinia felt relaxed. She felt content and at ease and happier than she'd been in years. Not the flashing, blinding happiness of a sudden triumph, an unexpected success. The calmer, steadier, longer-lasting happiness of no problems at the forefront of attention, no immediate worries, no self-doubts, no fears for the next moment or the next hour.

It was inevitable that Lavinia should compare Sandra with Greg, contrasting the effect each of these people had upon her. With Greg, Lavinia was self-consciously brittle, tightly restrained, artificial. With Sandra, she was totally unconscious of self. She felt natural and discussed subjects of interest to herself without having to worry about the listener's reaction to her views.

More than this. With Greg, she was a woman trying to keep a man, but unable to keep him with the methods and resources of a woman, forced rather to hold him with bribes. With Sandra, she was an individual in uncalculated conversation with another individual, with no advantage to be gained or lost by either party.

And now two hours had vanished, and the party was in diminuendo, the conversation finished. Lavinia didn't want the conversation to be finished. It was she who suggested that—if Sandra had nothing else planned, of course—they go somewhere for a drink. Sandra, apparently flattered and pleased that the editor-in-chief of *Milady* should be so friendly with her, agreed at once.

In the cab, it was Sandra who suggested they go to her apartment for the drink instead. Lavinia thought it was a fine idea. This was such a pleasant and agreeable girl. Sandra gave the cabdriver the new destination, an address on Grove Street in Greenwich Village.

Sandra's apartment was consciously not Bohemian. Candle-topped Chianti bottles, burlap drapes, dangling mobiles, torturous driftwood, all were conspicuously absent. The apartment contained three rooms; a long, narrow living room, a tiny bedroom and a tinier kitchen. The bath was down the hall, shared with the girl in the next apartment.

The apartment was done in what Sandra called "Salvation Army modern." An ancient, lumpy, sagging sofa, complete with faded flower-print slipcover, was the major piece in the living room, flanked by scarred drum tables and three widely unmatched living room chairs. The lamps and lampshades were uniformly horrible, and the domestic Oriental rug on the floor was a genuine relic.

The bedroom was completely functional. A three-quarter Hollywood bed with a yellow spread. A many-drawered dresser, age unguessable. A rung-backed chair. An oval throw rug.

The walls were bare, save for one painting, amateurishly framed and hung above the sofa. It was harshly colored and extremely nonobjective, and Sandra admitted, sheepishly, that it was her own work. "I got involved in that kind of thing for a little while," she explained. "I keep it to remind me not to weaken again. Isn't it horrible?"

(Later, Lavinia would remember that moment, and realize this was the warning, the indication that Sandra might not be as honest and motiveless as she seemed. Knowing Lavinia disliked nonobjective art, a calculating Sandra would also dislike nonobjective art. One doesn't hang a horrible reminder on the living room wall. Particularly when that is the only example of one's work placed on view. Later, Lavinia would realize this, but not now. Now, she was blinded—not by love, but by need. A need she wasn't yet aware of.)

Sandra made drinks, and Lavinia told her how cute her apartment was, and they discussed rents and apartment hunting and styles of furniture. They sat together on the sofa, and it seemed there was no limit to the subjects they could discuss, and it seemed amazing how often they were in agreement.

There was a small record player in the living room, and after a while Sandra put a stack of records on and tuned the volume down to the lower threshold of audibility. The music was many-stringed, slow dance tunes. Sandra came back to the sofa, and the conversation went on.

It was Sandra who started to hum with the music, and who said, "I wish I knew how to dance. You see people dancing, and it looks so easy. The closest human beings can come to just floating."

"You never learned?"

Sandra shook her head. "I don't know why. Just never got around to it."

"I used to like to dance," said Lavinia. What she meant was that she used to like her dancing partners. The thought reminded her of Greg, and she winced, and thought again of the long slope down which she was sliding, and that Greg was not the worst.

Sandra broke into her thoughts. "Do you dance well?"

Lavinia smiled, shaking her head. "I used to—"

"Would you teach me?"

"You mean, right now?"

Sandra jumped to her feet, a young and vivacious and totally innocent girl. "Why not? I'd love to learn, I really would. I can turn the volume up just a bit—nobody ever complains about the record player."

It was a silly idea, and Lavinia was ready for a silly idea. She was almost twenty again herself. This was almost a room in a college dormitory. "I don't know how good a teacher I am," she said, getting to her feet, "but I'm willing to try."

Sandra learned with surprising speed. She was graceful to begin with, and Lavinia only had to show her a step two or three times before Sandra was doing it as naturally as though she'd been dancing all her life.

It was fun at first, while they were stopping every other minute for Lavinia to explain or to demonstrate or to correct. And Lavinia found it confusing—and therefore absorbing—to be taking the male role in the dancing.

But after a while, when Sandra had a few basic steps down pat, and they could dance without interruption, suddenly it wasn't fun. It brought up too many memories. And every memory led to another memory, and the men she had known moved before her in a steady, downward, degrading procession, from that first man when she'd been too young, to Greg when she'd been too old.

And all at once she was crying. It was a stupid thing, she hadn't cried for years. But the drinks she'd taken, the loss of Greg, the dismal certainty of the future, the youth and friendliness of this girl Sandra, all combined and commingled, and she was sobbing against Sandra's shoulder.

They stood together in the middle of the room. Sandra's arm was around her waist, Sandra's other hand stroked her hair, Sandra's voice murmured in her ear: "It's all right. Cry it out. Lean against me. It's all right."

Somehow, they were sitting again on the sofa, and the music from the tiny record player was unbelievably sad. Lavinia threw off all restraints and all controls and became unashamedly maudlin for the first time in eighteen years.

It was so soothing, Sandra's arms around her, so comforting, Sandra's young breast to cry against. Lavinia had been held by many men, but no one had ever been so gentle with her, so calm and understanding with her.

And when Lavinia raised her face, streaked with tears, it was the most natural thing in the world for Sandra to hold her tight and to lean down and kiss her gently on the lips.

This was the danger point. This was the instant when Lavinia understood her actions and their direction. This was the time—and the only time—when she could have pulled away, ending it forever.

But no man's arms had ever been so warm, no man's lips had ever been so soft, no man's touch had ever been so gentle. Lavinia tensed, froze—then relaxed, closed her eyes, and drowned.

The kiss was long, and when they finally parted, to gaze searching in each other's eyes, Sandra whispered, "My Sappho."

"My Atthis," whispered Lavinia, and the pact was sealed.

It was the first time again. Twenty years had been stripped away and she was once more a virgin, coming for the first time, diffident and unsure, to her lover. Sandra caressed her, kissed her mouth and eyelids, her throat and cheeks, and the most wonderful thing was the gentleness of it. And she knew that this first time, there would be no pain.

Her body responded to the incredible lightness of Sandra's touch, and she clung to Sandra with a degree of passion that she had thought had long since been drained away. When they moved to the bedroom, it was Lavinia who undressed them both.

And Sandra's body was so exciting! So familiar, so intimately familiar, and at the same time so wondrously strange. It was as though Lavinia were fondling her own body of twenty years ago, a familiar self grown strange with time and circumstance.

Lavinia longed to touch, to kiss, to caress, to rub herself against that familiar stranger from the past. Sandra, in whispered monosyllables, told her the ways of this strange kind of loving. And suddenly Lavinia's timidity vanished. Her hands on Sandra's warm, naked flesh were as eager and demanding as were Sandra's on her own body. They drew closer and closer, legs and arms entwined, lips hotly joined, writhing in an ecstasy that transcended all feeling, all awareness . . .

Now, seated at her desk, Lavinia wondered why it had gone wrong, why Sandra wasn't the person she imitated so well that first night. And she understood, fully now, that Sandra was simply Greg again. But with a much stronger hold on her than Greg could ever have maintained.

She glanced again at the Miriam Staples Rider folder, opened it and leafed through the correspondence it contained. The letters to Sandra weren't there.

She hadn't really expected they would be.

2

IT WAS TEN-THIRTY before Anita Rawlins came to the dictator article in her in-basket. She looked at it blankly for a minute, wondering why it was back here again, and then read the typed note paperclipped to the manuscript. "I certainly agree that this is a terrible situation, but the subject matter is miles from our type of thing. Why not suggest to the author that he try one of the men's magazines? Maggie."

Anita felt angry, helpless and bitterly ashamed all at once. To think that *Milady* could find no place for the truth about this terrible, terrible dictator! It was wrong, wrong, wrong! And there wasn't a thing she could do about it, not a thing.

The editorial hierarchy at *Milady* was a high, narrow-based pyramid. At the bottom were the first readers, politely termed "assistant editors." There were three of these, including Anita Rawlins. Above them were the second readers and the third readers, assistant editors all. These people all had the same job; to cull from the mass of incoming manuscripts ones potentially usable in the pages of *Milady*. The slush pile—unsolicited manuscripts from writers unknown by the editors of *Milady*—went directly to the first readers, and three-quarters of it never got any farther. The first readers were well stocked with rejection slips. What they passed was then read by the second readers, who rejected about half, either with printed slips or brief notes. The third readers sliced the remainder in half again, and so on up.

Manuscripts from literary agents began their climb with the third readers. Manuscripts from writers known to the editors—writers such as Miriam Staples Rider and Alice Clothier—went immediately to the top of the pyramid.

The first, second and third readers—assistant editors—judged mainly by the criterion of readability, interest and literary value. Above these were the associate editors, who judged the relatively few manuscripts reaching them from the point of view of editorial policy, accepting only those manuscripts which were of the "*Milady* type." These finally reached Lavinia Cartwright's desk, where the actual selection for the magazine was made.

Anita Rawlins, therefore, was at the bottom of a rather long ladder. She could reject absolutely, but she could accept only conditionally, with the sure knowledge that most of the stories and articles she sent higher up would sooner or later be rejected anyway. This was disheartening, but at least some of the material she had read had already appeared in print in *Milady*, which gave Anita a prideful feeling of accomplishment, as though she herself had written the piece in question.

Only once, in the seven months she had worked as an assistant editor, had Anita come across a manuscript about which she felt a genuine passion. This was a factual article about a Central American dictator. The author, a college student and amateur writer, had spent the summer in the country, and had collected a fantastic amount of information on the dictator, all of it substantiated. In August, he had been forced to leave the country. He had immediately written the article and—for reasons best known to himself—had mailed it to *Milady*.

Anita had gotten the manuscript in the slush pile. She read with horror the documented record of torture and injustices and murder described by the author, and unquestioningly sent the manuscript on its way up the ladder. But this time she felt strongly enough about it to append a personal note to the second reader, outlining her own enraged feelings on the subject and expressing the hope that the second reader, too, would accept the article.

The note had carried the manuscript through both second and third readers, but the piece had foundered on the desk of the first associate editor to see it. Maggie Klein, whom Anita knew only slightly, had seen at once that this article would be grossly out of context amid stories of young love and news of the latest Paris fashions. But the note still served one last purpose. Rather than reject the article herself, Maggie had written her own note and sent it with the manuscript back to Anita.

And now Anita was supposed to reject it, and she couldn't. She didn't care about editorial policy, or about context. *Milady* was a national magazine, one with which she was proud to be associated, and it absolutely had to have a place for an article as important and as shocking as this.

That *Milady* would shrink from publishing this truth was unthinkable.

She considered talking to Maggie, trying to explain to her why the article should be accepted, but she knew that wouldn't do any good. Maggie was old in her job, and she wouldn't admit to being wrong even if Anita could—which was unlikely—prove to her that the article should be published. Besides, even if she convinced Maggie, there were other associate editors even farther up, any of whom might conceivably reject the article without letting Anita know about it.

She spent an hour worrying about it, chain-smoking and staring at the wall of her cubicle. She couldn't reject the article, she absolutely couldn't. Nor had she the power to accept it. Nor would it do any good to talk to Maggie.

It took an hour, but finally she built her courage up to the point where she acknowledged to herself the only possible action she could take. She would have to bypass Maggie, bypass all the associate editors, and bring the article directly to someone at the very top.

She was aware that such an action might result in her being fired, with the article rejected anyway. But there was the possibility she could talk someone into accepting it, and as long as that was a possibility, her course was clear.

Trembling but determined, she left her cubicle and headed down the long hall toward the executive offices at the very end. There she paused. In front of her was the office of Lavinia Cartwright, the editor-in-chief. To her right, Sandra Keel's office. To her left, Barry Sanderson's office, his title of managing editor on the door. It was to one of these three people that she must appeal, and she hesitated, wondering which would be best.

Lavinia Cartwright? Anita had met Miss Cartwright, for about a minute, the day she was hired, and hadn't exchanged a word with her since. She had heard already that Miss Cartwright was in one of her bad moods this morning, and it was common knowledge that she wasn't pleasant at the best of times. Not her.

Sandra Keel? There was something cold about Sandra Keel, cold and hard and unemotional. Anita's contacts with Miss Keel had been few, but they had been enough to convince her that she would never be able to like the woman. Not her.

Barry Sanderson? He was the only man on the editorial staff of *Milady*. He kept pretty much to himself, but he always had a pleasant smile when he and Anita passed in the hall, and none of the girls had anything bad to say about him. Besides, he was a man. He would undoubtedly understand this article, and why it should be published, more than either woman. He was the one to talk to.

Anita braced herself, trying to be calm, then pushed open the door and marched in. She strode on by Mr. Sanderson's secretary, toward the door to the inner office. The secretary said, "Mr. Sanderson doesn't want to be disturbed—" But it was too late. Her hand was already on the doorknob, turning, and she was in his office.

Barry Sanderson, nursing a hangover, studied the row of pill bottles on his desk. Miss Enright had left a glass of cold water in easy reach of his right hand and had tiptoed out, gently closing the door behind her. And now he studied the row of pill bottles, trying to decide which one to use.

"Eeny meeny miny mo." His hand touched one of the bottles. He spilled out two grooved yellow pills, popped them into his mouth, and followed them with water. Without warning his door burst open.

Startled, he looked over the top of the glass at the intruder. He saw a young girl, twenty-one or -two, youthfully slender, auburn-haired, bloused-and-skirted, and wearing an expression of terrified determination.

"What's this?" he said, and put the water glass down.

"I've got to talk to you Mr. Sanderson. It's important."

He recognized her, now. A first reader, Anita somebody-or-other. He pawed at random at the papers on his desk, saying, "I'm rather tied up at the moment, Miss Uhhhh . . . maybe Miss Enright could help you, or—"

"It's important," she repeated, and the desperation in her voice reached him through the hang-over. "You're the only one I can talk to."

He stopped pawing, and studied her again, wondering what was wrong this time. That was the thing about working for a magazine like *Milady*. Barry Sanderson was a lone man in the middle of a gaggle of girl editors, and there was little in life he disliked more than a girl editor. Particularly one of these empty-headed fluff balls, straight from a New England girls' college and bursting with sincerity.

Sincerity in an editorial office, as far as Barry Sanderson was concerned, was like a bathing suit at the North Pole. Nothing particularly wrong with it, but nothing particularly useful about it either. And Barry Sanderson—he told himself—ought to know. Thirty-six years of age, he'd worked in the publishing business for eighteen years, on every kind of magazine from men's adventure to tiny tot coloring books. He'd written, edited, done layout, sold space—anything and everything.

Milady was, for Barry Sanderson, both a step up and a step down. It was the first slick magazine he'd been connected with, and the highest pay check he'd ever drawn. And the job was one of the easiest in the world. A page and a half of *Milady,* every month, was devoted to milady's hubby, the theory being that the husband eagerly read these pages, then leafed through the rest of the book, and noticed the ads. That's what the advertisers were told, at any rate. A page and a half a month. And since no husband would be caught dead with a copy of *Milady* in his hands, Barry could do pretty much as he pleased. He was reasonably sure he had no readers. And he didn't have a thing to do with the rest of the magazine. Just that page and a half.

At the same time, it was rather embarrassing to have to admit that one worked for a magazine as unflinchingly feminine as *Milady*. It was like a male ballet dancer, or an interior decorator.

In reaction to this, Barry had unconsciously grown more aggressively masculine in the year and a half he'd been working for *Milady*. He drank more than he used to, his voice was deeper than it had been, and his words had acquired just the faintest tinge of a Hell's Kitchen accent. Although he didn't realize it, this metamorphosis to a rough, tough Barry Sanderson had been one of the contributing reasons for the failure of his marriage. After eight years, Dorothy had left him, winning her divorce a month ago. The new Barry Sanderson couldn't cry about it.

But the weekends were hell—empty and intolerable without Dorothy—while his Monday morning hangover was becoming an institution. Miss Enright now knew that Barry should be left completely alone on Mondays, so he could spend hours playing soldier with his pill bottles on the green desk blotter.

Then suddenly there was this quivering young girl in his office, clutching what looked like a short manuscript and staring at him with stricken-fawn eyes. Barry looked at her, and sighed. "Trouble?" he inquired, in the forlorn hope that she would answer, "No," and go away.

Hopes shattered. She said, "It's this article. I passed it, and Rhoda passed it, and Janice passed it, but Maggie wants to reject it, and we *can't!*"

He squinted. Did this little idiot really think he'd bothered to memorize the *names* of that squadron of simps out there? "Rhoda?" he repeated. "Janice? Maggie? Can't what?"

"I'm first reader—"

"I know what you are."

"And . . ." She faltered, looked around helplessly like a television actor who can't locate the prompter card, and suddenly lunged forward to shove the article at him. "Just read it," she said. "You'll see what I mean. We *can't* reject it, we *can't.*"

He took it. There wasn't much else he could do. Once it was in his hands, he automatically started to read it.

It was rough going for a hung-over Monday morning. The thing was twelve pages long, and he got through four pages before he had to put it down, swallow two more pills, and think about something else, hard.

The girl—Anita Whosis—had been watching him intently all the time he read. Now she said, "Do you see what I mean? People ought to *know* about things like that."

"I—see your point," he said. He studied the girl through half-closed eyes. A recent college graduate, full of hopes and ideals, sincere as Saint Francis . . . Old, rusty feelings and emotions and ideals of his own stirred in sympathy with her, understanding the degree of courage it had taken to barge into his office with this thing. The subject *was* a bitter and important one.

But the hung-over Barry Sanderson wanted no part of it. And the editorial Barry Sanderson understood just how great the chasm was between this article and the format of *Milady*.

What could he say to her? She would never be able to accept the impossibility of it, not at her age and with that light burning in her eyes. "You Can Change The World." Oh, yea?

It was too much for him. He passed the buck. "I'm not the one to see," he said. "I know what you mean about this article. I find myself agreeing with you about its importance. But I don't select the non-fiction. Miss Cartwright would be the one to talk to, Miss Uhhh . . ."

"Rawlins."

"Miss Rawlins. You see Lavinia Cartwright. She's the only one who could help you." He held the article out to her, avoiding her eyes. "I'm sorry," he said.

"Miss Cartwright?" She sounded scared.

"She's the only one who could help you."

"I see. Well—thank you."

"Not at all. I'm sorry I can't do anything for you."

"Yes. Thank you."

He watched her back out of the room, and the thought crossed his mind that he was probably sending the poor little broad off to get fired. Well, he thought, that's one way to learn. Maybe the only way. He lined up the pill bottles for the war.

Anita had now gone too far to stop. And, surprisingly, invading Lavinia Cartwright's office proved a lot easier than invading Barry Sanderson's. Maybe only because she now had practice at it, and felt more self-confidence. After all, she *had* talked Barry Sanderson into reading the article, and he *had* agreed with her. She didn't doubt his words or his motives at all, accepting his flat statement that only Lavinia Cartwright could give the final okay for the article.

She sailed by Miss Cartwright's secretary with no trouble at all, and found the editor-in-chief standing by the window, looking down at the rushing taxis on Park Avenue. "Miss Cartwright—"

Lavinia Cartwright turned and looked at her. Framed by the light square of the window, the older woman's face was dark and thin and deeply lined. One plucked eyebrow raised, as she studied Anita, face, clothing, posture, hairdo, manuscript . . . "What is it?"

"This article." Anita wished fervently for the eloquence of Cicero. But all she could think of was the old advertising gizmo, the testimonial. "Mr. Sanderson read it, and he agreed with me, but he said you were the only one who could decide."

The lines of Miss Cartwright's face shifted, to produce a puzzled smile, and she walked across the room to her desk. Her walk was graceful, thought Anita, graceful and economical, like a fashion model's walk. Anita envied women who could walk well. In college, she had been one of the worst people in the posture class.

"Do I know about this article?" asked Miss Cartwright as she sat down behind her desk.

"No, not yet, but—"

"Come to think of it, do I know you?"

"I'm Anita Rawlins, Miss Cartwright. I work up front. I'm one of the first readers."

"Oh, yes. And this article?"

"I talked to Mr. Sanderson—"

"You wrote it, is that it?"

"Oh, no. I passed it on, and so did Rhoda and Janice. The second readers, you know."

"I know them." She nodded, closing her eyes, and the faint smile was still on her lips.

"But Maggie rejected it, and I knew it wouldn't do any good to talk to her—"

"So you talked to Barry Sanderson?"

"I didn't know who to see about it. I've never done anything like this before."

"How long have you been with us?"

"Since March."

"Seven months. You understand what your job is supposed to be?"

"Oh, yes, Miss Cartwright, I—"

"And you understand what Maggie Klein's job is?"

With a sinking heart, Anita recognized the echo of teachers, dorm proctors, parents, in Miss Cartwright's voice. She nodded. "Yes."

"Maggie's been with us for a long time. Twelve years, I think. She knows her job, Anita, believe me she does. I haven't seen Maggie wrong yet."

"But this time—"

"What is it, a short story? Maybe one of our other magazines—"

"It isn't a story, it's an article. It's—" But she knew she lacked the author's eloquence. She couldn't do the article justice in a one-sentence synopsis. Beseechingly, she held the manuscript out. "If you could just look at it, you'd see why we have to publish it. We *have* to!"

The eyebrow raised again, and the smile became a bit broader. "We have to?" She took the article, a bit gingerly, and set it face up on her desk top. She glanced at the title, the author's name, and the first paragraph, and her smile faltered. She turned the page, read a bit more, and the smile disappeared, replaced by a frown of bewilderment. As she leafed through the manuscript, the frown deepened. Then she leaned back in her chair, and looked at Anita again, still frowning, and said, "Well, I—"

Anita saw no understanding in that frowning face. Miss Cartwright hadn't really read the article, she'd just skipped through it. She hadn't seen the force and the importance of it. Anita leaned forward over the desk, forgetting to be tongue-tied. "Don't you see? That terrible man—those poor beaten people—if people *knew* this was going on—"

"Yes, but—"

"Public opinion," said Anita, as though she were uttering a talisman. "People could write to their Congressmen. He suggests that at the end of the article."

"Yes, I saw that."

"There could be a trade embargo," said Anita, remembering the words the author had used. "The United States could refuse to deal with that man, could stop all support—"

"Anita, believe me, I see the point. But *Milady*—after all—"

"But don't you *see?* We have more readers than practically anybody. We're one of the top five magazines in the country in number of readers. And the readers are women. Women always feel more strongly about injustice and brutality than men do. What other magazine could tell the story to so many people? Where else could this story find as big an audience?"

Lavinia Cartwright didn't answer her for a moment. They stayed frozen, like a movie still, Lavinia sitting back in her chair, frowning up at the girl, Anita leaning over the desk, sincere and impassioned.

Then Lavinia Cartwright moved. She shook her head, and the frown was replaced by the puzzled smile. "You've thought this all out, haven't you?"

"Yes, of course. When I first saw the article, I was so *proud* to be working for *Milady*, because I knew *Milady* was the perfect magazine for it, and I'd read it before anybody else."

Miss Cartwright's smile broadened, and she reached out to pat Anita's hand. "You're a sweet girl," she said. "How old are you?"

"Twenty-two."

"Where's your home town?"

"Norwalk, Connecticut."

"Is that where you went to college?"

"No. Sanders College, in Rhode Island."

Miss Cartwright nodded. "I used to know some girls from Sanders." She picked up the article, held it as though weighing it. "This really means a lot to you, doesn't it?"

"Oh, yes, Miss Cartwright. I couldn't believe Maggie would reject it."

"I understand why she did." She smiled again, nodding. "Yes, I understand why. Editorial policy, you know."

"But—"

"Hush. Let me think a minute."

Anita subsided, and stood biting her lower lip, an action which lessened her apparent age from twenty to sixteen. Miss Cartwright, carrying the article, got up from her desk and strolled back to the window. She stood looking down at the street, and after a minute she murmured, "Quite a bit different from Central America, isn't it?" She motioned at the scene beyond the window and smiled at Anita.

"All the advantages we have," said Anita.

"Yes." She stayed at the window a minute longer, then moved back to the desk, walking around to the front of it, to stand next to Anita. She dropped the manuscript on the desk, and took Anita's hands in hers. "You were afraid when you came in here, weren't you?"

Anita smiled sheepishly. "Yes, I was. But I just couldn't let it be rejected. I couldn't."

"You're a sweet girl," said Miss Cartwright again.

"Tha-thank you."

"Don't let New York spoil you, Anita. Don't—" She paused, then shrugged, looked away, and released Anita's hands. "You came to work in March," she said, as though to herself. "How strange that is. Just around the time—Well, no matter." She was suddenly brisk and business-like. "You leave the article with me. I'll have to think it over. It would be—quite a departure for us."

Anita let out a breath she hadn't known she was holding, and felt her body relax for the first time in fifteen minutes. "Thank you, Miss Cartwright," she said. She took Miss Cartwright's hand in both of hers, held it tight. "Thank you so much."

Miss Cartwright raised her free hand and patted Anita's cheek. "You're the freshest thing that has happened to me in years," she said.

It was on this tableau—Anita clasping Lavinia's hand, Lavinia's other hand touched to Anita's cheek—that Sandra Keel entered.

"Ready for lunch, Lavi—"

Miss Cartwright moved suddenly away, seeming to be flustered and confused for just a second. Then she was immediately business-like again, saying, "You leave the article with me, Anita. I'll read it over more carefully. And I'll definitely let you know my decision, one way or the other."

"Thank you, Miss Cartwright. Thank you again."

"I'll be with you in just a second, Sandra," said Miss Cartwright, and Anita knew she had been dismissed. She left the office happily, hardly noticing Sandra Keel as she brushed by her, and half-skipped down the hall to her own cubicle.

Miss Cartwright would publish the article! Anita was sure of it. The woman had promised to read it more carefully, and when she did she couldn't possibly want to reject it then. Not possibly.

It was a triumph. It was more of a triumph than anything that had ever happened in Anita's life before. More than getting good grades in school, more than getting a particular dress or coat, more even than getting this job in the first place.

And Miss Cartwright had been so nice, so understanding and sympathetic. And Mr. Sanderson, too. The both of them, they were such *nice* people!

Anita wished there were someone she could share her triumph with. But her roommate, in the apartment on West Forty-sixth Street, was an actress, and away now with a touring company. She wouldn't be back until the beginning of November. If her parents had been home, she could have called them in Norwalk, but they had celebrated Anita's independence by finally taking that trip to Europe and wouldn't be back in the States until just before Christmas.

She had to talk to somebody. She considered Rita or Alice, the other two first readers, but she was afraid that might be misconstrued. After all, she'd gone over Maggie's head, and Maggie wouldn't like that at all. And it would only make it worse if it looked as though Anita had been bragging about it afterward.

But she absolutely had to talk to somebody. She couldn't keep it in, she could hardly sit still at her desk.

She finally thought of Barry Sanderson again. He'd been such a pleasant person, and he'd taken an interest in the article. She could call him, tell him how her interview with Miss Cartwright had gone. He'd probably want to know.

If anyone from anywhere else in the world tried to contact Barry Sanderson in his office, by phone, Barry Sanderson's secretary would be the one who would answer. But the telephone on Anita's desk was "inside." All she had to do was dial his extension number, and instead of the phone ringing at the secretary's desk, *his* phone would ring.

There was a stenciled sheet, giving the extension numbers for all the editors and subeditors, Scotch-taped to the side of the desk, near the phone. Anita studied it, found Barry Sanderson—fourteen—and dialed.

He answered almost at once, saying, "Don't *do* that. My head hurts."

"I'm awfully sorry, Mr. Sanderson, I didn't know."

"Is this Miss Enright?"

"No, sir. This is Anita Rawlins, Mr. Sanderson, and—"

"Who?"

"Anita Rawlins. I was talking to you this morning about—"

"Oh. Oh, yes, the Central American dictator."

"That's right. I just wanted to thank you for being so patient with me."

"That's perfectly all right. Any time."

"And I wanted you to know what Miss Cartwright said. I thought you might be interested."

"You went to see her?"

"Well, yes. Sure. That was what you said."

"So I did. And?"

"She didn't say definitely yes, but she liked it."

"She did?"

"Didn't you think she would?"

"Well, uh—I wasn't sure."

"She wants to read it over again." Anita was having a hard time restraining herself, staying impersonal and businesslike. "I think she's going to publish it. I really do."

"Well, that's fine, uh, Miss Rawlins. Fine. Congratulations."

"Thank you."

"The next time I have some bright idea of my own, maybe I'll get you to do the presentation for me. You seem to have the touch."

Anita couldn't hold it back any longer. She laughed out loud.

"Well, uh," he said, "I'll be talking to you." He hung up and looked from the phone to the battleground on his desk. "A nut," he whispered at the pill bottles. "A certifiable nut."

Sandra smiled at Lavinia, and motioned at the door through which Anita had just exited. "Interested?" she asked, mockingly.

"Don't be silly," said Lavinia, but a dull flush colored her cheeks.

"I won't," said Sandra, and her smile was grim.

3

IT WAS NINE-TWENTY, the elevator doors slid open, and Lavinia glared out at the stenos, who, she knew, had been working furiously for all of half a minute. She stalked through them to the green door and beyond, to Editorland.

An open door on her left as she walked down the plasterboard-partitioned hall gave her a glimpse of Anita, in a classic pose, profiled, head bent slightly as she read, graceful neck swan-curved, a tiny pulse beating in the throat. Lavinia's glower deepened, and she walked on.

Twenty-four hours ago, Anita had not even been a name. This morning, she was—a problem.

What was she going to do with that bloody article? Totally unfit for *Milady*, but to reject it would be to reject Anita.

And what was she going to do about Sandra? Sandra, last night . . . Her slyness was now as transparent as the stalking of a snake. "Let's go right home from work, Lavinia. I haven't cooked dinner for us in weeks."

No, by God, you haven't.

Lavinia nodded to the crisp good morning of Miss Henderson, continued into her own office, removed her coat and settled behind her cluttered desk. Manuscripts to read, article queries to reply to, artwork to choose from, correspondence to answer—she tried to get to work, but she couldn't. In the back of her mind was Anita, and that savage article, and a decision to be made. In the front of her mind was Sandra, and last night, and another decision to be made.

Dinner by candlelight, with Sandra chattering constantly. If Lavinia hadn't known her so well it would have been a beautiful job of acting. The chatter was half shop talk—"The hat layout was fabulous. I never in the world thought anybody could get seven pages out of a new style of hat." And half propaganda—"I don't mean to be bitchy, Lavinia, I really don't. But I'm jealous, that's all there is to it. Every time you look at another girl, I just go green. I couldn't bear to lose you, dear."

Lavinia had remained mostly silent. She had responded to the shop talk, when she absolutely had to, but she had been silent to the propaganda. There was nothing to say, that was all. Throw Sandra out? She'd love to, she'd really enjoy it. But she wouldn't enjoy being alone. And daydreams of Anita were, after all, only daydreams. She was not, from the looks of her, a girl to be easily seduced by anyone, either man or woman—especially not by a woman.

Throw Sandra out? Not without someone to replace Sandra. Living with a bitch was still far better than living alone.

They went to bed early, and Sandra was more loving than she'd been in months. Caressing her, kissing her, whispering of love. Before tonight Lavinia would have closed her eyes and sighed and let the warmth of Sandra's touch drown out all thought. But tonight there was the final knowledge that this affair with Sandra was ending. Because tonight Lavinia looked beyond the soft caressing, the murmuring and the satin-smooth writhings of their naked bodies on the bed, and she saw Sandra's eyes cold and watchful in the darkness, and knew the love-making to be a lie.

But she said nothing. Sandra was false, hard, and merely using Lavinia. But Sandra was still better than a life alone. And so she went through all the motions, kissing and being kissed, suffering Sandra's knowing hands upon her breasts and belly and thighs and eventually responding with violence to the insidious rise of passion inside her.

Now, Lavinia stared unseeing at the cluttered desk, a manuscript opened but unread in front of her, the work still piled up, nothing done. The short, hard staccato of the telephone jarred her, and she started, blinking, taking a few seconds to come back from last night and the faces of Sandra and Anita to today and the desk and the telephone, which rang again.

She reached out for the phone suddenly, quickly, as though she were late for something important, and her voice was unnecessarily loud when she said, "Miss Cartwright."

"Jake, Lavinia," said the masculine voice. "Could you come on upstairs for a minute? No rush. Whenever you're not busy."

"I can come up now." To talk to someone—anyone—about something—anything—was the only way to snap herself out of this depressing post-mortem.

"Fine," he said, and hung up.

Jake Stoneman, owner of Chalmers-Mead Publications, had his office on the floor above, almost directly over Lavinia's office. To walk the length of the building to the elevator, wait for it to arrive and take her up one flight, and then walk back the length of the building to Jake's office was more trouble than it was worth. Four years before, an executive stairway had been built, connecting the three floors leased by Chalmers-Mead. The stairway was to the right of Lavinia's office, and could be reached only from her office and Barry Sanderson's. She took this stairway now, wondering what Jake wanted, and every step upward was at the same time a mental step backward in time.

God, I'm retrospective this morning, she thought, and pushed away the memory of the Lavinia Cartwright and the Jake Stoneman who had lived and loved eighteen years ago. They're both dead, she told herself fiercely. Jake's married now, he's been married for fourteen years. And Lavinia has gone dyke.

A sword of self-revulsion, carefully shielded, slipped its scabbard now for one second to stab deeply to the exposed nerve of her lesbianism. She grimaced and thought quickly of something else, anything else. Sandra. Anita. Jake.

Jake at twenty-seven and Lavinia at twenty-two, and the world still teetering on the edge of the Second World War, not yet toppled by the appearance on stage of the United States. Jake, a depression baby from a neighborhood one shaky rung above a slum. Lavinia, one year out of a private girl's college in western Massachusetts. Jake, whose Orthodox parents had given him up when it became clear that financial success was his only god. Lavinia, whose Long Island parents had given her up when she ignored their list of eligible potential husbands and announced that she was going to be a career woman. (What a dangerous and exciting phrase that was then—a career woman! What the phrase *soldier of fortune* was to men, the phrase *career woman* was to women. What a naive, pretentious, silly, unprepared little fool she had been, with her sixteen years of education and her unshakable belief that a misty strange thing called "independence" was the panacea for all her troubles!)

She had reached the top of the stairs, and the unmarked door to Jake's office. She knocked, once, and he called to her to come in.

Jake Stoneman at twenty-seven had been an individual, thin, nervous, bitter, driving, sharp. Jake Stoneman at forty-five had softened to a type. He had grown heavy, his black hair had thinned irregularly, revealing a soft pale scalp, and his face had thickened with good food and discontent. He looked like half the wealthy men in New York, and the similarity went deeper than his looks. He thought as they did, dressed as they did, voted as they did. He owned what they owned, a pale cream Cadillac and a brick home on the Island and an apartment in town and a cottage at Miami Beach.

On his orderly, uncluttered desk stood a small clock, shaped like the wheel of a sailing ship, and Lavinia was startled to see that it was quarter after ten. Almost an hour she had spent, downstairs, brooding. That was unlike her, and it worried her.

Jake said, "What about this Sandra Keel, Lavinia?"

"Sandra?" Whatever she had expected, it had not been to come upstairs and hear the name she had been brooding over below. "What about her?"

"How much authority have you given her?"

Lavinia sat down slowly on the maroon leather sofa. Was this the Miriam Staples Rider thing? Or had Sandra overstepped herself somewhere else? What was she going to *do* about Sandra?

"The ordinary authority," she said. "She's my assistant. Why? What did she do?"

"She was just up here. Did you give her the right to hire and fire?"

"Of course not." It was only too clear! Sandra firing in order to put in people who would be loyal to her rather than to Lavinia. It couldn't be tolerated. She would have to tell Sandra firmly that it couldn't be tolerated, that she had gone too far. "Why?" she asked, trying to be casual on the surface. "Whom did she want to fire?"

"One of the first readers." He read the name from a slip of paper. "Anita Rawlins."

"Definitely not!"

The vehemence of it surprised them both. Jake looked at her with surprise. "I haven't done anything about it," he said. "I told her I'd have to check with you."

"I'll take care of it," said Lavinia. She had herself under control again, the voice volume down, and when she stood she didn't tremble. "Thanks, Jake. I'll handle it."

"What is it?" he asked her. "One of these personality conflict things?"

"Yes, that's all. I'll handle it."

"Better get rid of one of them. There's no time for squabbling around here."

"I will. You can depend on that."

He peered up at her and said, "What's the matter with you, Lavinia? Going to miss a deadline?"

"I never have yet," she said.

"You're upset about something."

"It's this—squabble. They're both good workers. I hate to have to fire either of them."

"It's up to you. But don't let it get you down."

"I won't." She looked at him, not wanting to leave yet, not wanting to have to go downstairs and act, but at the same time not wanting to talk with him about Sandra or her own upset any more. She looked at him, and inside the softness and the extra weight and the affluence she caught a glimpse of the Jake who was twenty-seven years old and reaching out to snap the world in two. "Jake," she said.

"What?" It wasn't the twenty-seven-year-old Jake who asked that. It was today's Jake, the publisher, and she didn't have anything to say to him.

She shook her head. "Nothing, Jake," she said. "Thanks for telling me about Sandra."

"It's your bailiwick, Lavinia. I told her that."

"I'll take care of it, Jake," she said, and realized she'd already said it too many times. "I'll do it now," she said, and escaped from his office.

Going back down the stairs, she fastened on the memory of Jake at twenty-seven, as the least painful of all the thoughts crowding her mind and jostling for attention.

They'd both been working for Palmer Publishing, a frantic, understaffed outfit with a long line of pulp magazines. Westerns, detective, romance, fantasy, Western romance, adventure, any and every kind of pulp. It was this job that had finally caused her parents to give her up, to ask her gently but firmly to not come home any more. To be a career woman was bad enough. To work for an organization that published such trash was unforgivable.

One day, when she'd been working there three months, Jake Stoneman made his sudden appearance. He was like that then, fast and sudden, sharp and bitter. He hadn't found his niche yet, but he was looking. He was looking hard.

He stayed four months at Palmer Publishing, reading, writing, doing some layout work, faking letter columns. He and Lavinia discovered an instant dislike for one another. To Jake, Lavinia was a soft-life rich girl, slumming among the working stiffs. To Lavinia, Jake was a crass pusher, nervy and jangling.

Lavinia had done most of her work with the romance magazines, and she had been engaged in an uplift campaign of which she herself was hardly aware. Consciously, she ignored the opinions of her parents, and told herself that a job was simply a job. Unconsciously, she tried to turn the love pulps that were her livelihood into something closer to her parents' standard of approval.

Jake put an end to that. He darted into her cubicle, waving the latest issue of *Exciting Love Stories,* and shouting, "What is this crap? What do you think this is, the *Kenyon Review*?" He had gone on like that, insulting her, screaming at her, jabbing a thin finger at the magazine.

She had white paste sticky on her fingers. She'd been pasting up galley sheets. When she slapped him, some of the white stuff clung to his bony cheek.

He didn't hesitate. He slapped her back, harder than she had slapped him, hard enough for her ears to buzz. "Now we've slugged each other," he said, in a calmer tone, "maybe we can talk."

She switched to his weapon, words. "What business is it of yours—"

"The Old Man told me to," he said quickly. "Sales on *Exciting Love* are down thirty percent under last January."

That fast statistic had ended the battle. She sat down again at her desk, and he talked to her, for an hour, while she listened. He told her the facts of life involved in the publishing of a love pulp, and she paid close attention. She also paid attention to the fact that he knew what he was talking about, that he would always be a man who would know what he was talking about. That he might have chosen to let her be fired instead of talking to her this way.

When he asked her to lunch, she went. When he asked her to dinner, she went. When he asked her home, she said no. He thought it was because she was a virgin, but she'd stopped being that four years before, as a freshman in college. In a canoe, awkwardly and ludicrously, with a boy who knew no more than she did. And male sex would always be, thereafter, slightly funny to Lavinia Cartwright.

Almost always. For she didn't say no forever to Jake. They went out together, to dinner, to the movies, to an occasional play. First she came to respect his drive, then she came to like his bitter honesty, and finally she came to wonder what it would be like to go to bed with such a sharp, hard bundle of nervous energy.

It was an explosion. She had been to his two-room West Side apartment before, but she had always stopped his advances, and he had been willing to wait. She was introducing him to music, to Beethoven and Tchaikovsky and the recent radical, Stravinsky, and they listened that night to *The Rite of Spring*. He always wanted to know what the music was about, what the composer was trying to say or to describe. When she told him that *The Rite of Spring* was about pagan fertility rites, he nodded and said, "He got it, then. Not like that whatchacallit, Ravel. You know, the *Bolero*. It isn't like that, steady and even. It's like this music here. It's harsh and jumbled. It rips you to pieces."

She smiled at him. "You're so sure you know everything, aren't you?"

"I'm sure of sex," he said, and looked at her, his mouth a thin, grim line. He studied her while the music thrashed on, and then he said, "You're staying here tonight."

The smile was suddenly brittle on her face. "What makes you think so, Jake?"

"Because we both want you to."

"You're sure you know me, too, is that it?"

"I know you," he said. "You've been waiting for me to ask you."

"Not this way."

He shrugged. "What difference does it make? This is the way I'd ask you. You want me to make believe I'm one of your Long Island boyfriends?"

"You don't have to be ashamed of yourself, Jake."

"You're right," he said. "I don't." He got to his feet, switched off the record player and all the lights but one, then came back to stand in front of her, one hand extended for her to take. "Come on," he said.

She was trembling. His face was in shadow in the semi-dark room, but she could see the harsh angularity of his body as he stood in front of her, the thin, long-fingered hand extended. "You don't love me," she whispered. "You don't even like me very much."

"I want you," he said.

The trembling was getting worse. He wanted her, and she wanted him. She couldn't understand why. He was ugly and crass and brutal, but she wanted him as she'd never before wanted any man. She raised her hand to his, and he pulled slightly, helping her up from the sofa.

They took one step toward the bedroom, but she was weak, as though she'd been sick for a long time. She leaned against him, closing her eyes, and he put his arms around her. "I'm so weak," she whispered, and they tumbled together to the floor.

He was quick, harsh. He scraped her clothes away, his lips were bruising against hers, his hands were rough on her flesh, his body was bony and hurting. But he was as practiced as he was rough, and his fingers on the taut, aching mounds of her breasts, and on the smooth planes of her thighs, and soft curving mound of her body awakened a hot tide of desire in her. This time as the hard spear of his passion found the secret core of her being, she was lifted out of herself and shaken like a rag doll. Something was tearing her apart, searing and burning her and she was left limp and weeping on the hard living room floor, Jake lying again beside her, his breath hot in her ear, his hands now gentle on her bare, quaking flesh.

For the first time in her experience of him, he was not harsh. "Don't cry, Lavinia," he whispered. "Vinnie, don't cry. It's all right." And she knew that in some strange way she had conquered him, too.

Later, they could smile at each other, and he could say, "I have a perfectly usable bed in the other room, you know."

And she could answer, "I do believe I'm going to walk with a limp for the rest of my life."

She stayed that night, and the second time, in bed, he was gentler, and they took the time to savor and appreciate one another, to know the *who* and not just the *what*.

They never lived together, but she spent two or three nights a week at his place. They didn't share an apartment, because they were both afraid. Both still young, both still clutching tightly to that new-earned possession, independence, both unwilling to expand their plans and desires and ambitions to include another person.

Then the world toppled into the Second World War, and Jake pulled some strings. He wouldn't be an infantryman, he would work in Washington, in Army public relations. Their goodbyes were brief, and neither of them promised to write. Independence was such a fragile thing, to be so jealously guarded. He left New York, and Lavinia refused to acknowledge the fact that she was in love with him.

They hadn't seen each other again until after the war, and by that time he was already married. He'd saved his money, bought into one of the new paperback book companies, sold at a profit and begun his own line of Western pulps. He got out from under just before the Western pulps met their sudden end, moved here and there within the publishing field, buying, selling, merging, working, until now he owned Chalmers-Mead and was soft and balding and rich, and the abrasive young Jake was only rarely visible deep within.

When he'd bought Chalmers-Mead, three years before, Lavinia had immediately turned in her resignation, not sure herself just why she had to leave, why she couldn't work for

Jake Stoneman. He had come to her apartment, to talk her into staying. When she had seen that he was now a different man, that the Jake Stoneman she had loved was no longer alive, she had agreed to come back to work. They were business friends now, and the past was never mentioned.

From Jake, through how many men, to Greg. From Sandra, to what?

To Anita. To someone, to anyone. But no longer Sandra, that much was clear. She had to get rid of one of them, fire one of them, Sandra or Anita. Sandra had forced the choice perhaps weeks before Lavinia would otherwise have made it. And once the choice was necessary, it was also inevitable what the decision would be.

Back in her own office, she touched the intercom switch, and told Miss Henderson to have Sandra come in. Then she waited, sitting behind her desk.

She had thought she would be frightened, nervous, when the final break-up came. Instead she was merely relieved. Throwing Sandra out wasn't going to be a chore at all; it would give her definite satisfaction.

Sandra took ten minutes to come from her office next door. She entered cool and calm, apparently sure of herself again, sure that her hypocrisy of last night had smoothed things between Lavinia and herself.

Lavinia began at once. "You tried to get Anita Rawlins fired. Why?"

Sandra shrugged. "Her work is poor. She passes completely unusable stories all the time."

"That's a lie."

Sandra looked startled for just a second, and then she smiled, a sheepish smile that would have fooled Lavinia a month ago, even a day ago. "You're right," she said. "It is a lie. I did it because I was jealous."

"You were afraid I might throw you over for her, is that it?"

"I thought she might try to worm her way closer to you, Lavinia. That's all."

"And you knew how easily that could be done."

Sandra came across the office, her face a bland smile of sincerity. "Honey, I thought that was all over. Last night—"

Lavinia made a nervous hand motion, interrupting her. "Never mind last night. You were lying then. You've lied to me for months. You've used me from the beginning."

"Honey, I never have!" With an air of shocked incredulity, the wounded lover stood crushed before the brute's desk.

"Jake told me I had to fire one of you," Lavinia told her coldly. "You or Anita Rawlins. From all I've heard, Anita Rawlins does perfectly satisfactory work. She has never caused me any trouble. Your work has been less and less satisfactory lately. You've caused me a good deal of trouble. I've decided to keep Anita Rawlins."

The incredulity this time was real. "You're going to fire me?"

"Completely. As of this minute. When I get home to-night, I want your things out of the apartment. Otherwise, I throw everything down the incinerator."

"You can't do this!" The shock was still real, as Sandra tried to understand that she could go too far after all.

"I'm doing it, Sandra. I'm through with you. I don't want you around. I don't ever want to see your face again."

Sandra opened her mouth to speak, then closed it again. Lavinia watched the expressions that flitted across her face, from shock to disbelief to rage to cunning, until the face was suddenly blank again, wiped clean of emotion, and Sandra was back in control of herself. "It wouldn't do any good to tell you about my feelings for you, would it?"

"No, it wouldn't."

"Or to promise that I'll do better in the future."

"There isn't any future. Not with me."

"Lavinia, I hate to say this, but I'm afraid I'll have to appeal to Mr. Stoneman. And of course I'll have to tell him the full facts in the case."

Lavinia's smile was wintry. "You mean if I fire you, you'll tell Jake that I'm lesbian. Is that it?"

"I'll have no choice, Lavinia. I don't want to hurt your career that way, but—"

Lavinia shook her head. "Forget it. Jake and I were bedmates before you were using sanitary napkins. He wouldn't believe you. He'd laugh you out of his office."

Sandra hesitated, as though wondering whether or not to believe that, and then she said, "Mr. Stoneman isn't the only one—"

"If you open your mouth about me," Lavinia said, cutting her off, "I'll see to it that you never get another illustrating job in New York."

Emotion showed once more on Sandra's face. Raging hatred, cold and bitter. "You'd blacklist me?"

"You know I would. And you know I can. If you want to keep on working as a commercial illustrator, you'll keep your mouth shut about me. Nobody in the world knows about us except you and me. If it gets out, you'll be the one who did the talking. And I'll keep you from working in New York."

Sandra was now shaking with rage. Her eyes were narrow and hate-rimmed. "I'll get you, Lavinia. I swear I will."

Lavinia knew herself superior to this snarling girl, knew herself to be the victor. "Be melodramatic somewhere else," she said, reaching for one of the manuscripts on her desk. "I have work to do."

"I'll *kill* you!" The black plastic pen-stand from Lavinia's desk was suddenly in Sandra's hand, and Sandra's face was now viciously red as she hurled it at Lavinia's head.

Lavinia ducked instinctively, one arm going up to shield her face, and the pen-stand struck her forearm, jarringly, and fell onto her lap upside down, ink pouring out onto her dress.

Lavinia got to her feet, the pen-stand rolling away onto the floor. Now, at last, she felt belated fury at this girl who had used her, lied to her, played her for a fool. "I can beat you that way, too," she said coldly. Kicking off her high-heeled shoes, she came around the desk toward Sandra.

Sandra backed away, confused and desperate. "Lavinia, I didn't mean to," she stammered. "We don't have to end this way. I do love you, Lavinia—"

Lavinia slapped her ringingly across the face, forehand and backhand, and Sandra stumbled and would have fallen but that she came up jarringly against the wall. Lavinia stepped forward to slap her again.

Sandra shrieked, "Leave me *alone!*" and rushed out from the wall, bowling into Lavinia and sending them both toppling to the floor. Lavinia squirmed away, hampered by her tight skirt, got to her knees, and struck out at Sandra again, wild ineffectual open-hand slaps, until Sandra rolled away.

They were both crying and gasping, both trembling from their violence. Lavinia was the first to recover enough to be able to talk. "Get out," she said, forcing the words between gulping breaths. "Get out for good."

She went back to her desk, picked up the pen-stand and saw that it was wet with ink, dropped it into the wastebasket, and sat down to look ruefully at the ink-stained mess that was her skirt.

She didn't look up until she heard the door open and close. Sandra was gone. Lavinia was too nerve-taut to know what her reaction was.

She calmed slowly, and when she was sure she could talk without gasping, she called her secretary on the intercom. "There's been an accident, Miss Henderson," she said. "I've spilled some ink on my skirt. Go out and buy me a dress, will you? You know my size, the kind of thing I like."

"Yes, Miss Cartwright," said Miss Henderson, who must have noticed the condition Sandra was in when she left the office, but who would never mention it.

Lavinia next picked up the telephone, dialed Jake Stoneman's extension. "I decided," she told him, "to get rid of Sandra Keel. She just couldn't learn how to accept responsibility."

"I had the feeling she wasn't our type of person," he said, and she reflected again how much he had changed from the old Jake.

"I really should have released her some time ago," said Lavinia.

"Do you have anyone on the staff in mind to take her place? Or should we start looking around?"

"No, I've got someone in mind," said Lavinia, and smiled at the phone as the thought deepened to certainty. "Anita Rawlins."

4

BARRY SANDERSON was working late. Not, he told himself firmly, through any desire to talk to Anita Rawlins. It was simply that he had a lot of work to do.

Which was bushwah. All right, he wanted to talk to Anita Rawlins. He wanted to find out what the hell was going on.

He had the strange feeling that he was out of touch with the world. Something had zipped by him unseen, and now he was trying to catch up and figure out just what the hell it was.

He went through it one more time in his mind. On day number one, one of these giddy girl graduates had bounded into his office, wanting to mount a crusade against Latin America or something. He had side-stepped, passing her on to Lavinia, knowing full well there was a dandy chance the idiot would get fired. On day number two, Sandra Keel, Lavinia's assistant, got fired. And the giddy girl graduate took her place. And scuttlebutt had it that the atrocity article was going to be published, good God.

Now, just what the hell had happened? In twenty-four hours, this kid zooms from a first readership to editorial assistant, with a pay check equal to Barry's and a responsibility five times as great. And Sandra Keel, who was a bitch but otherwise ignorable, is out on her can.

It had been a week now, seven full days, and Barry still hadn't figured it out. With a page and a half of *Milady* to fill once a month, this left him plenty of time to kill in one way or another, and he had been killing time the past week trying to understand this rags-to-riches saga in the office across the hall. Lavinia was being close-mouthed, Lavinia's secretary was being close-mouthed, Anita's secretary was being close-mouthed. That left nobody but Anita herself.

So here he was, at five-fifteen, still in the office. And he was usually gone by four-thirty. Miss Enright had left at five o'clock, Lavinia and her secretary had gone home, separately, at about the same time, Anita's secretary had gone home a couple minutes later. And Anita, new at her job and hopelessly sincere, was still working.

Barry had both doors open, the one leading to Miss Enright's office and the one beyond it leading to the hall. From his desk, he could look through to the closed door behind which Miss Horatio Alger was still puttering away. He picked up his pencil, fought himself to a draw at yet another game of tick-tack-toe, when—click!—the door across the hall opened, and the Success Girl appeared.

Barry surveyed her sourly. Her arms were full. She was toting a purse, an attaché case and a large, well-filled manila envelope. She was taking work home, for God's sake!

She was preoccupied, and didn't see him watching her. Closing her office door, she walked out of his line of vision, down toward the elevators.

Banzai! He crumpled and threw away the paper filled with tick-tack-toe, shrugged into his topcoat, closed doors behind himself as he went, and advanced to meet the Mysterious Lady at the elevator.

As he walked down the hall, he wondered how to go about it. Prying for information just wasn't one of his talents. He finally decided, as he pushed open the green door leading to the steno pool and the elevators, to simply come right out and ask her.

She was standing by an elevator, schoolgirl-looking with her armload. She smiled at him and said, "Hi, Mr. Sanderson."

"Barry," he told her gallantly. "We are equals now. May I carry some of that?"

"Thank you, yes," she said with relief, and let him take the attaché case. "It does get pretty heavy."

He held an imaginary microphone up before her face and said, "Tell me, Miss Anita Rawlins of Podunk, Puxatawny, to what do you attribute your sudden rise in the editorial world?"

"Eating Wheaties every day," she said, and giggled.

His smile sagged at the corners. That approach had fallen flat on its face. Time for the "we boys" gambit. Or would it be "we girls"? "No, seriously," he said. "I've never seen anybody leap to prominence quite as rapidly as you did. You got important friends or something?" He knew that was a safe question. Chalmers-Mead based its hiring on ability, not on important friends. It was the only way to get people who knew what they were doing.

"I guess I must have," she said, still smiling back at him. The smile turned into a slightly puzzled half-frown, and she said, "I really don't know myself what happened. I talked to Miss Cartwright about that article, and she said she'd think it over—"

"I remember. You called me about that."

"That's right. Then, the very next day—"

The elevator came, and the conversation halted while they stepped aboard. Then she started again. "The very next day, Miss Cartwright called me into her office—in the afternoon, when I came back from lunch—and asked me questions about what I would do if such-and-such happened, and what I would say to a writer who said such-and-such to me, and all at once she told me I had the job." She giggled again, which Barry found an extremely annoying habit, and shrugged her shoulders. "I still can't really believe it. I didn't expect it for a minute."

"And you don't know what made her choose you?"

"I can't even guess. The only time she'd ever even met me was the day before, when I talked to her about that article."

The elevator stopped at the first floor, and they walked together through the lobby and out to the street, crowded now with late shoppers and workers hurrying home. "I'll walk you to your subway," he said.

"Oh, I don't take the subway any more," she said, and once more she giggled. The giggle was really an atrocious sound, but she did look good while she was doing it, there was no denying that. Eyes bright, lips curled in a lovely smile. If only the sound were less grating.

The giggle stopped, at last, and she said, "I take a cab home now. After all, I'm making so much money. I feel like a millionaire or something, taking the cab home every night."

Barry was suddenly sure that this kid really did eat Wheaties every day. With sliced bananas. And that she really didn't know what accident of the gods had given her this new job. "I'll snag one for you," he said, and stepped off the curb to wave at passing taxis.

One stopped, finally, and Anita bundled aboard, among her luggage. "Thanks a lot, Mr. Sanderson," she said, looking out at him.

"Barry," he reminded her. "First names. They go with the cabs and the big salary."

"I forgot," she said, and giggled once more. "I still can't believe it." Then she gave the driver her home address, on West Forty-sixth Street, and the cab surged belligerently out into the traffic.

Barry repeated the address aloud, to remember it— though he wasn't sure exactly why he wanted to remember it—and turned uptown. Except for the giggle, he thought, Anita Rawlins was a very pleasant young kid. Just a young kid, of course. And completely crazy. But pleasant.

Anita's apartment was a fourth-floor walk-up two blocks west of Times Square. There were three rooms, cluttered with furniture. Some of it had been there to begin with, some of it had been brought in by Anita's roommate, some of it belonged to Anita. There was a single bed in the back room, where the roommate slept when she was in town, and a studio couch in the living room, which was Anita's bed. The roommate now being out with the touring company of

A Sound of Distant Drums, Anita had taken over the bedroom in the interim.

With her roommate away, the apartment was suddenly much larger, and much emptier. Anita knew no one in New York, except for her co-workers at *Milady* and her roommate. The roommate had tried introducing her to a few boys, but they had all been heavy-breathing Beatniks or egotistical young actors, and Anita found herself bored with them very soon. The co-workers were strictly that, co-workers, with lives of their own, and none of them had invited her to join their circle of after-work friends. It was neither that they were callous nor that Anita was unlikable. New York is the city of instinctive privacy, and it is often difficult to bridge this convention and give friendship a chance to get started. She and the other girls were great pals at the office, but only at the office.

The evenings, therefore, were long. It hadn't been so bad when the roommate was in town. They could talk together, simply be in the same room together, reading or whatever, and the fact that there were two of them cut loneliness to a minimum. But now the evenings were very long indeed. Anita had tried club-joining, with no success at all. She had paid thirty dollars to join a cinema club, whose members gathered every Sunday afternoon at a Greenwich Village movie house to watch confused, amateurish and not-very-interesting noncommercial films. But none of the other members (most of them middle-aged and recently prosperous) ever spoke to her, and after a while she stopped going. Since she owned a camera, she joined a camera club. The people here talked almost constantly, but only about cameras and photographs, and most of them were frayed, frustrated little people, blinking behind eyeglasses, and no fun at all to be with.

So now she stayed home every evening, and did a large amount of reading, record-listening, and television-watching. Also, she wrote long letters to the few friends she'd made at college, none of whom were in New York, and spent hours cooking elaborate meals for one.

With the new job, she had found a new evening activity. She read manuscripts at home, or she did some of her correspondence at home, on her portable typewriter. She knew Mrs. Marshall didn't like her doing her own typing, but she did it anyway.

Actually, the new job was embarrassing in some ways. Mrs. Marshall was old enough to be Anita's mother, but instead Anita was her boss, and that was an awkward relationship indeed. Mrs. Marshall didn't seem to mind, called Anita "Miss Rawlins" with no obvious discomfort, did her work as she had always done, but Anita was terribly ill at ease giving orders to a woman old enough to be her mother.

The job itself was mostly letter-writing. Letters came in from agents and from writers and from readers, and Anita's job was to answer them all. When a letter confused her, as sometimes happened, she took it to Miss Cartwright—whom she was now supposed to call "Lavinia," though she could never remember to—and Miss Cartwright—Lavinia—would tell her what to do.

She also did some copy-editing, correcting structural mistakes in sentences, fixing typographical errors, and eliminating objectionable phrases. If an author said something derogatory about a product advertised in *Milady's* pages, Anita changed the remark. If an author used a word that made Anita reach for the dictionary, Anita changed the word.

Then—most nerve-racking of all—she sometimes had to confer with illustrators. She and the illustrator were supposed to discuss the story, the amount of space which would probably be given the illustrator, and decide what the illustration should look like. Anita let the illustrators pretty much have their own way, since she was certain that they knew a lot more about the subject than she did.

Tonight, she had brought home with her two short stories, an article on dieting, and two letters that had to be answered. One of the letters was rather important, and she got at that immediately after dinner.

It was a letter to a writer named Miriam Staples Rider. Miss Cartwright—Lavinia—had told her what the circumstances were. Sandra Keel had managed to annoy Miriam Staples Rider, and Miss Rider had sworn to never submit her stories to *Milady* again. Lavinia had written to her, telling her that Sandra Keel was no longer working for *Milady,* and today an answer had come, grumbling a bit, to the effect that Miss Rider wasn't convinced that all was yet well with *Milady.*

So Anita, as Sandra Keel's replacement, was to answer the letter, to show Miss Rider just how different she was from Sandra Keel, and how much better things were at *Milady* after all. "Be tactful," Lavinia told her. "Tell her how much you've always liked her stories, and that you hope to be working with her on stories in the future, and that you'll certainly see to it that nothing like the Sandra Keel incident ever crops up again. Lay it on thick, but not too thick. After all, she writes for a living, and she can tell if you're overdoing it."

So this one Anita would take her time with. She had read a lot of Miss Rider's stories and serials, and honestly did like them, so there wasn't any trouble there. She'd just reread her letter one more time, and then do a first draft of her reply.

While she was reading the letter, the doorbell rang. She wondered if her roommate had come back to town unexpectedly, because the show closed or something, and then realized the roommate had a key and wouldn't be ringing the downstairs bell. Who else would be coming to see her?

The bell rang again, and Anita hurried across the room to press the buzzer, hoping it wasn't going to be another of those charity-drive people. She could never refuse somebody from a charity drive, but there were so many of them these days that after a while a person began to feel imposed upon.

She opened the peephole in the door and peered out at the stair well, listening to the sound of a woman's high heels coming up the stairs. The woman rounded the turn at the second-floor landing, and Anita saw that it was Sandra Keel. Now, what in the world did Sandra Keel want here?

She wondered if the girl thought that Anita had been to blame for her losing the job. She hoped not, hoped the woman wasn't going to make a terrible scene. She wished she could make believe she wasn't home, but she'd already answered the bell, so there wasn't any way out.

She opened the apartment door as the woman reached the top of the stairs, and was relieved to see that she was smiling. So it wasn't going to be an uncomfortable interview after all.

"Hello, there," said Sandra. "Can I come in for a minute?"

"Sure," said Anita. She stepped back out of the way, and closed the door after Sandra had entered.

Sandra looked around at the cluttered living room and said, "What a charming little place!"

"It's in kind of a mess right now," said Anita apologetically. "Can I take your coat?"

"I can only stay a minute," said Sandra, removing the coat. "Taking work home with you? My, you are industrious."

"I'm still learning the job," said Anita self-consciously, as she hung Sandra's coat in the hall closet.

"There isn't so much to learn, really." Sandra settled herself comfortably on the studio couch, sitting relaxed with her back against the wall, and smiled at Anita. "It's just a glorified correspondence secretary, that's all."

"It seems a lot more than that," Anita told her, "after being a first reader." She sat down in the basket chair across the room from Sandra, and wondered when the woman would get to the point.

"I did want you to know I don't blame you for my being fired," Sandra said. "Lavinia and I just had an—argument, that's all, and she got mad and fired me." She shrugged, smiling, as though it really didn't matter, and said, "It was my fault, actually. I'd been rather undiplomatic with one of Lavinia's favorite writers."

Anita was about to say that she knew about it, that as a matter of fact she had just been reading a letter from that particular writer, but then she thought better of it. Sandra apparently didn't begrudge her the job, but there was no sense rubbing it in. So, instead, she said, "I'm glad you don't blame me. I didn't know anything about it until you were already gone."

"Oh, I know that. I'm not blaming you at all." She looked around at the living room again. "Do you live here all alone?"

"Right now I do. My roommate is touring with a hit play at the moment."

"Oh, you room with an actress!" Sandra said it as though it were both the most surprising and most delightful bit of information she'd ever heard. "That must be fascinating." she said. She was smiling and animated, as though she had no purpose visiting Anita other than to chat, and Anita wondered if that could possibly be true. But she hardly knew Sandra Keel at all. The woman had to have some reason for being here, and Anita waited awkwardly for Sandra to get to the point.

But Sandra seemed content to chatter on, about nothing at all. "Do you have any interest in acting?" she asked.

"I'm afraid not," Anita told her. "I was in a play at school once, and I was awful."

"I've always thought," said Sandra, "that it must be fascinating to be in the theater. Making millions of dollars, being worshiped by your fans, with your slightest wish instantly obeyed." She smiled again at Anita. "Don't you think that would be nice?"

"I guess it would," said Anita. "My roommate isn't like that, though."

"Anita," said Sandra, all at once serious, "I hate to ask you, bother you or anything, but it was rather chilly outside and—well, do you have any instant coffee or anything like that?"

Anita, embarrassed at not having thought to offer Sandra something to drink, got quickly to her feet, saying, "Oh, I'm sorry. Of course. I'll get it right away."

"No, no," said Sandra, standing up. "Don't trouble yourself, I can get it. I don't want to be a bother, really."

"It's just instant. I can get it."

They wound up preparing the coffee together, getting in each other's way in the tiny kitchen. Through it all, Sandra kept on chatting aimlessly about acting and the apartment and the weather, and Anita kept wondering when the woman would get to the point.

She finally did as they carried their coffee cups into the living room. "Come sit by me," said Sandra. "I want to talk to you, seriously."

"All right."

They sat down on the studio couch and put the coffee cups on the end tables. Then Sandra covered one of Anita's hands with her own, and said, "I'm glad Lavinia gave you the job. I was afraid she'd be so mad at me she wouldn't do it, because I'd been the one who recommended you. But Lavinia isn't the type to let personal feelings interfere at the office."

Anita felt herself gaping. "You recommended me?"

"Didn't she tell you? No, I can see why she wouldn't. Yes, I told her about you, only a day or two before I—left. Not in relation to *my* job, of course. I didn't know I'd be leaving so soon." She smiled briefly, to show that the loss of the job was no longer painful, and went on: "But I did tell her you were by far the best of the new girls in the office. Maggie Klein had recommended you to me, and I passed the recommendation on to Lavinia."

"Well—thank you . . ." Anita didn't know whether to call her Sandra or Miss Keel, and she fumbled to a halt.

Sandra seemed to understand the problem. She squeezed Anita's hand slightly, and said, "Please call me Sandra. I want us to be friends. I never did get a chance to know you very well at the office, but I did want to. May I call you Anita?"

"Yes." Anita returned the other woman's smile, suddenly liking her, thinking that the coldness she had so often displayed at the office hadn't been her true self at all. A lot of women were like that, Anita told herself, self-consciously cold while at work in an office, but much nicer outside.

Sandra squeezed her hand again, and said, "I want us to be friends, Anita. It's so difficult to make friends in this city."

"Yes, I know. I don't know anybody, practically."

"You know me. We could be good friends, Anita." Her other hand now rested on Anita's knee, lightly, and she said, her voice low and solemn, "It's so terrible to be all alone. No one to talk to, no one to share things with, no one to love."

"Yes," said Anita. The warmth and closeness of the woman were pleasant, comforting. The hand holding hers, the hand resting gently on her knee, Sandra sitting so close to her, it was all soothing and good. Anita was surprised and pleased that this woman wanted to be her friend, and she was also grateful.

"I'd like us to go everywhere together," Sandra was saying. "I'd like us to be the closest of friends."

"I'd like it, too," Anita said, and squeezed Sandra's hand.

"Maybe we could even find an apartment together," Sandra said, as though the thought had just occurred to her.

"If your roommate wouldn't mind, if she could find some-one else to move in with her."

"She's practically never in town anyway," Anita told her. "She wouldn't mind."

"Are you a good cook? I'm a terrible cook."

"I'm a wonderful cook," Anita said, laughing with pleasure.

"Then you do all the cooking, and I'll do all the dish-washing. Agreed?"

"Agreed."

"And we won't be lonely any more, either of us." Sandra put her arm around Anita's shoulders, and her other hand pressed more firmly on Anita's knee. "We'll share every-thing, go everywhere together. We'll even share the same bed, sleep every night with our arms around each other."

Anita's smile faded, and she frowned in confusion. "Sleep together?"

"Why not? Like a pajama party, every night. Didn't you ever go to a pajama party?"

"Sure," said Anita doubtfully.

"What's wrong?" Sandra asked her. "There isn't any-thing wrong with it, if we want to sleep together, if we want to sleep with our arms around each other all night, if we want to kiss each other sometimes."

Anita felt a fluttering nervousness starting in the pit of her stomach. Something had changed, the conversation had shifted, the companionship that had sounded so wonderful was suddenly strange, frightening. "I don't think I'd like to kiss a girl," she said, trying to understand Sandra, trying not to hurt her feelings, trying not to think that she meant any-thing more than a pajama party, than simple friendship.

Sandra smiled again, her arm tight around Anita's shoulders. "Why not?" she whispered. "It's much nicer than kissing a man."

And suddenly she had pulled Anita against her, and was kissing her, her lips warm and bruising against Anita's, her tongue pushing and probing into Anita's mouth.

For the first few seconds, Anita was too stunned to move. Sandra's lips and tongue, Sandra's arm tight around her, Sandra's hand stroking her bare thigh beneath the skirt, it was all too sudden and too unbelievable.

But it was happening. Anita twisted her head away, pushed at Sandra with trembling hands, and forced herself free from Sandra's arms, up and away from the studio couch, gasping and wide-eyed and terrified.

Sandra was up and after her, face smiling, voice soothing, arms outstretched. "Don't run away, Anita. There's nothing wrong with us kissing. What could be wrong with two girls kissing?"

Anita knew now what this woman was. In college, in Greek literature, they had studied some of the poems of Sappho, the woman poet from the island of Lesbos in the Mediterranean. Love poems, from Sappho to her beloved, Atthis, who was also a woman. And the island, Lesbos, had given their love its name. Lesbian. They had been lesbians—homosexuals—with a strange dark twisted love that was filthy and obscene.

And Sandra was one of them. Sandra was a lesbian. Anita backed away, staring at her, as Sandra moved forward with soft, soothing voice and outstretched arms, and the wall was at Anita's back.

She hurled the name like a javelin. "Lesbian!"

Sandra stopped in the middle of the room, no longer smiling. "What does it matter what they call us?" she said bitterly. "You liked my arm around you. You liked my hand on your leg. You liked me to kiss you. What does it matter what name it has? You *liked* it."

"I didn't!"

"You wanted me to kiss you. You want me to come get you now, to kiss you again, to throw you on the floor and tear your clothes off!"

"Lesbian! Lesbian! Lesbian!"

"Stop that screaming!"

Anita ran to the hall door and flung it open. "Get out!" she cried, shaken and trembling. "I'll call for help—I'll scream if you don't get out!"

The bitterness in Sandra's face was deeper now, and she let her arms fall to her sides. "Why do you think you got my job, you little idiot?" she said angrily. "Lavinia wants you for herself. You won't turn *her* down, though. Oh, no, you won't turn her down. You want the precious job too much."

Anita stared at her. "What are you talking about?"

"You know exactly what I'm talking about."

"Miss Cartwright isn't like that. You hate her, that's all, because she fired you. Because she found out what you were. You probably tried the same filthy things with her, so she threw you out."

Shockingly, Sandra laughed, a harsh sound, jangling in the small room. "You really think so? Just wait and see."

"Get out of here," said Anita, struggling to keep her voice level. "With your filthy mind and your filthy lies, get out of here."

Sandra grimaced and turned away, to get her coat from the closet. She came back, shrugging into it, and glared at Anita as she left the apartment. "Just wait," she said.

Anita slammed the door in her face and leaned against it, spent. She couldn't remember when she'd been so terrified or so shaken. It was the way she might have felt if she'd just teetered off balance at the edge of a cliff and only barely managed to keep from falling: trembling, weak with fear, her mind in chaos.

After a minute, she crossed the room to the studio couch and sank down on it. She picked up her coffee cup and emptied it, even though the coffee was now cold. Slowly, she calmed down.

She'd never met a lesbian before. She'd never really believed in their existence. They were only Greek myths, like the gods of Olympus. To think that such people were real, and that Sandra Keel was one of them . . .

But not Lavinia Cartwright. That had only been Sandra's hatred and vengefulness talking.

All at once, she found herself wondering what on earth lesbians could do together. Sex with a man she understood, at least in theory, although she had never experienced it herself. But how could a person have sexual relations with another woman? What could they do together?

She stopped that line of thought with determined suddenness. That kind of curiosity could get her into trouble.

Not that there was any chance of her ever trying to satisfy that curiosity, certainly not with anyone like Sandra. Sandra was so bitter and harsh, vindictive and obscene. There wasn't any chance of Anita ever doing anything like that, she told herself reassuringly—not if all lesbians were like Sandra.

5

IT WAS FRIDAY AGAIN, and the party was supposed to start at six. Lavinia frowned as she thought of it, thinking again of the fact that she wouldn't be able to go home and change first.

Why did people call these things cocktail *parties?* A party was the last thing it was. Everybody standing around, jockeying for position, whispering slander to each other, looking for a pickup, hoping to be still sober when the victim was drunk and winding up drunk anyway. And somebody would get too loud and somebody else would fight and somebody else would throw up and somebody else would make a play for somebody else's wife.

She hated having to go to these things, but there was no way out of it. "Just put in an appearance, Lavinia," Jake always said.

Well, Anita would be going along with her to this one, so at least she'd have someone to talk to. And maybe tonight . . . She grimaced at the thought. For over two weeks now, ever since she'd put the girl in Sandra Keel's job, she'd been trying to make the first pass, the first suggestion. But the time had never been right, the mood had never been appropriate, Lavinia's courage had never been sufficient, and the words had remained unsaid.

The phone rang and she glanced at her watch. Ten to five. It couldn't be anything important this late in the afternoon. She picked up the receiver, and a male voice identified itself as Bob Larson. Bob was editor of *Epic*, the true-men's magazine in the Chalmers-Mead group. "About that atrocity article you sent down here, Lavinia," he said. "I just finished it, and I can use it all right. It's a well-done piece of reportage."

"Thanks a lot, Bob," she said, and smiled with relief.

"God knows why he sent it to you."

"He should be just as happy to be published in *Epic*."

Lavinia put the receiver back in its cradle, and smiled again. That took care of that. She'd been sitting on the article for the last two weeks, not knowing what to do with it. She couldn't publish it, not in *Milady*. But she couldn't reject it either, because that would end all thought of a relationship with Anita forever. This way, Lavinia was off the hook, and Anita should be just as happy.

Maybe tonight after all, she thought.

Anita looked out the cab window at the crowds. She'd been riding cabs twice a day now for more than two weeks, but she still wasn't used to it, she still gawked out the window like a teenager or a tourist. But she didn't care what she looked like. It was fun to be riding in a cab and staring out the window at the crowds.

And tonight the cab was going somewhere special. Not to her empty and lonely apartment way over beyond Ninth Avenue, in a very unfashionable section of Manhattan. Tonight, she was going to a cocktail party, an actual cocktail party. On Central Park East, no less, where all the embassies were. And she was going with Lavinia Cartwright, who was editor-in-chief of *Milady*, and they called each other by their first names. She wasn't even going to try to be cool and sophisticated about the whole thing.

"Anita," said Lavinia suddenly, beside her in the cab. "By the way . . ."

Anita turned to look at her, inquiringly.

"About that article, Anita. You know, the one about the dictator."

"Yes?"

"It just wasn't right for *Milady*, I'm afraid—much too far from our normal kind of thing." Lavinia stopped and laughed at the open-mouthed shock on Anita's face. "Don't look so terrified," she said, patting her knee. "I didn't reject it. *Epic* is publishing it. I showed it to Bob Larson and he snapped it up right away."

"*Epic?*" Anita was trying to think, trying to compare *Milady* and *Epic* for size of audience, respectability of reputation, importance of content. She was hampered by the fact that she knew absolutely nothing about *Epic* at all.

"It's a very big magazine," Lavinia told her, as though she could read Anita's mind. "It's one of the top three men's magazines in the country. The article will be seen by just as many people as if it were in *Milady*."

"Oh." Anita was glad the article was going to be published, but a bit disappointed that *Milady*—her magazine—

wasn't going to be the one publishing it. But, she told herself, that wasn't the important thing. The important thing was that it would be published. "I guess it's more aimed at men anyway," she said.

"Of course it is," said Lavinia.

They smiled at each other, a crisis passed, and the cab turned out of the park onto Fifth Avenue.

The party was just as bad as Lavinia had expected. No, it was worse. It was probably the worst party she'd ever attended, the one for which the word "party" was most completely a misnomer.

The occasion was the imminent publication of a novel by a woman writer who had appeared quite often in *Milady*, and Lavinia was at the present time dickering for the magazine rights to the novel, condensed and cleaned up. It was a working-girls-from-bed-to-bed book, to be its publisher's major item on the fall list. The trade papers were already drenched with full-page ads for it, with book dealers being offered the "one free for every ten you order" deal. The dealers, recognizing bestseller build-up when they saw it, were ordering like mad. The volume of their orders was so great that it was guaranteed a berth on the bestseller lists the week it was published. It seemed ridiculous that a book could be called a bestseller before any reader had ever bought it, but that was the way the system worked. Bestseller lists reflected the publisher's sales to book dealers. Readers of the bestseller lists, assuming that the lists referred to those books which had sold the most copies to readers, rushed right out to buy their own copy, so that a bestseller became a bestseller because it was already a bestseller.

At any rate, the party reflected the book. It was loud and it was flamboyant and it was sexy. Most of the cocktail parties Lavinia had reluctantly attended had been sexy, but in a quiet manner, with propositions being made in undertones in distant corners of the living room. This party was a good deal wilder. The propositions were fairly shouted across the room, and the bedrooms in the rear of the apartment were getting a strong play. And it was scarcely six-thirty in the evening! Lavinia thought this distasteful, like drinking before lunch. If these people couldn't wait till ten or eleven o'clock to hop into bed together, well, it was just in bad taste.

She sat alone in a phony Louis Quatorze chair, in the corner of the living room farthest from the door. She had expected to have Anita to talk to, to make this party a bit more bearable, but the girl hadn't been able to sit still. It was her first such affair and she had almost immediately run off, dashing here and there, nibbling on hors d'oeuvres, listening to bits and pieces of all the conversations scattered through the apartment. Lord knew where she was by now. Lavinia wondered if she was in one of the bedrooms, but rejected that at once. The girl was too wide-eyed innocent for that kind of thing. Particularly at six-thirty in the evening.

One of the liveried waiters passed by, with a tray of martinis, and Lavinia waved her empty glass at him. He came at once, and she traded the empty for a full. Six-thirty, she thought, with a different meaning this time, and looked at the drink. How many of them had she had, in the half-hour she'd been here?

She neither knew nor cared. Those couples in the bedrooms were disgusting. Why couldn't they wait, at least till the proper hour for indecent behavior? She giggled at the thought, and a fleeting image of Sandra making love to her crossed her mind. She swiftly emptied the martini glass.

Anita was in the kitchen, crammed between the refrigerator and a wall, more or less defending her virtue. A tall, heavy, black-mustached man, smelling of gin, leaned heavily against the refrigerator and pawed at her in an offhand manner, while he discoursed on Hawaii.

"Hawaii," he said again, "is not what it's cracked up to be." His roving hand made contact with her breast, and she pushed it away, flushed and embarrassed, wishing she could get out of this corner. "It's a tiny bunch of islands with a tiny bunch of towns on it," he said as he groped for her breast again and missed. "You think Honolulu is a metropolis or something? Big as New York, maybe, big as Chicago? Poo!" he said, and the gin breath came strong with the word. "It's a little dinky town. Smaller than Albany, for Chrissake. Smaller than Westport. Littler than Tarrytown, for Chrissake." His palm brushed her belly, slid downward to her pelvis and she flinched back against the wall, pushing his hands away. They looked like two lushes playing "Peas Porridge Hot," hands weaving and shoving in the narrow air between them.

Anita, who had given up answering his monologue minutes ago, looked helplessly over his shoulder, praying for somebody to come rescue her. Waiters streamed blandly by, carrying drinks to the living room and empty trays back to the kitchen, without so much as giving her a glance.

"Hawaii," he droned and clamped two hands on her breasts, "is not what it's cracked up to be."

She got rid of the hands again, and saw a chink of daylight between his body and the wall. She made for it, but he thrust himself against her, rolling his hips against her body. "You wanna dirty boogie?" he murmured.

"No," she said, and there were his hands again, one high, one low.

She could concentrate on removing his hands, or she could concentrate on pushing past him and getting to the kitchen doorway, but she couldn't concentrate on both. She decided on the doorway. With a quick, darting movement, she managed to get by him, he goosed her, which hurt. But she made it to the hallway, and was away from him at last.

The hallway was long, with the living room at the far end of it. Shouts and laughter and squealing came from down there, and the small segment of the room she could see was crammed with people who all seemed to be doing the dirty boogie.

This wasn't what she had expected from a New York cocktail party. Friends had told her about parties they'd been to, where famous writers or poets or sculptors or composers sat around and said disrespectful things about education, the government and everybody present, but this party wasn't like that at all. This was more like a Roman orgy, and Anita didn't like it a bit.

Not, she assured herself, that she was a prude or anything like that. But this was a far cry from the healthy sexuality of a fraternity dance or a beer party at college. These people were frantic and shameless, acting as though sex were nothing more than an entertainment, like the movies, which they were compelled to pursue to keep from being bored to death. They had all apparently been bored for years.

She wondered if they acted like this all the time, but she didn't see how that could be possible. Yet they had come here, started to drink and talk and laugh, until something happened, something electric that was in the air, and now they were carrying on like pigs.

She heard lurching steps behind her, and knew the mustached man was lumbering after her. At the same time, at the end of the long hall, a reeling man emerged from the living room, spied her, and with a shout of "Hi! Ho!" started toward her.

She couldn't go through that again, she couldn't just keep fighting off drunks for the rest of the night. She moved to the nearest door leading off the hallway, opened it, slipped into a semi-dark bedroom, and closed the door behind her.

There was a couple on the bed. She stared at them, frozen motionless with the fear that they would hear her, see her, know she was there and think she was spying on them like a novice voyeur.

But they were oblivious. They lay on top of the bedspread, naked and uncovered, and they were making love. The man was mumbling in a steady monotone, and after a minute she realized that he was counting, slowly and steadily, to the rhythm of their movement on the bed. "Sixty-*three*, sixty-*four*, sixty-*five*, sixty-*six*—"

It was too much. She wanted to scream, she wanted to cry, she wanted to run forever. The faces of the man and woman were in shadow, their bodies pale in the lamplight. They were sick and obscene and degraded, and she couldn't stand them.

Then she saw another door, off to the right. It couldn't be a closet door, because the closet was to her left, its open door revealing dresses and skirts hung in a row.

She crossed the room, quickly, trying not to look at the couple on the bed, and pulled open the door. It led to a bathroom, and a further door led to another bedroom. She went through, closing both doors behind her. Thank heaven, this bedroom was empty. She sat down on the bed, to try to collect her shocked emotion.

It was then that she remembered Lavinia. She'd run off and left her almost the minute they arrived, and she recalled that Lavinia had said she only wanted to stay half an hour or forty-five minutes.

A clock on the bedside table said five minutes past seven. And they had gotten here at six o'clock. An hour and five minutes. She must go back to the living room and find Lavinia.

While she was still making up her mind, the hall door opened and a couple started into the room, arms circling one another's waists, leaning on each other for support and grinning foolishly, as though they had started smiling for a reason at first, then forgotten what it was and just left their grins plastered on their faces.

They got one step into the room before noticing Anita, getting off the bed. "Whoops!" said the man. "Pardon us."

"It's all right," said Anita. She avoided looking at the woman. "I was just leaving."

"Oh," said the man. He had started to back out of the room, lugging the woman with him, but now he reversed his movements and came on in. He looked at Anita, at the bed, and around the room. "Alone?" he said, incredulously. "What are you doin' in here all alone?"

"Never you mind her," said the woman. She was a blonde, but Anita didn't know what she looked like, because she wouldn't look directly at her.

The man chuckled and shook a finger at Anita. "Nasty, nasty," he said. "You ought to get yourself a nice man, stop doing things all by yourself that way. Now, go wash your finger and be a good girl, you hear me?"

Anita felt her face go beet-red with embarrassment. The man laughed again, and she thought that now he had the idea his filthy suggestion was true, because she'd blushed. With the two of them looking at her, the man still laughing, she felt uncontrollable tears welling up in her eyes. She blinked rapidly, but they wouldn't go away, and she wouldn't let this animal see her cry.

Brushing by him, she ran out of the bedroom and down the hall, toward the living room and Lavinia.

Lavinia closed one eye and decided to focus on the fat redhead in the green knit dress. It was a game she was playing. She picked some red fathead—fat redhead—closed one eye, and tried to focus. When a waiter swam across her field of vision, she raised her empty glass and waved it, and he always came and took it from her and gave her a full glass in return. Then she played the game again, until the next waiter swam by. And the waving glass was always empty.

A few minutes ago, she had known she was drunk. Now, all she knew was that she was having a hell of a time focusing on the red fathead. The fat redhead. The head fatred. The fed hatred.

Someone came in close, so close it was absolutely impossible to focus on her, and said, "Lavinia! Lavinia, it's ten minutes after seven. Do you want to leave now?"

She opened the closed eye, closed the opened eye, peered upward at the too close figure. "Sandra?"

"It's Anita. Do you want to go home now?"

"Anita. Oh. Oh, yes, Anita." It was Anita, and she was going to take her home. Wasn't that nice? "I think that's lovely," she said.

"What?"

"I think we ought to go right home."

That led to a series of impossibilities. Standing up, for instance. She knew how to stand up, she'd been doing it all her life, but this time her knees just weren't doing their part. But finally they did, and she was standing, ready for the next impossibility. Walking across the living room to the front door.

Firm hands on her arm steadied her, and Anita—lovely girl, ought to sleep with her sometime—was asking her if she felt all right. "Perfectly lovely," she said, and navigated the living room and the hall, and came to a stop in the elevator. Whoosh! went the elevator, and she thought she was going to up-chuck, but she didn't, and then they were walking again.

It was dark out, and Anita rolled down the cab windows and asked Lavinia her address. She asked the second time, and Lavinia suddenly realized the girl was talking to *her*, so she answered.

When the cab moved, a chill breeze came in the near window, and Lavinia found her head clearing a bit. Just enough to let her realize she was tired enough to die. She closed her eyes,

and the cab grumbled and rocked comfortingly. Then suddenly it came to a stop. She tried to make believe it hadn't
stopped, by refusing to open her eyes. But Anita was talking
to her again, poking her shoulder, which was an annoying
thing for her to do. Reluctantly, she got out of the cab. The
doorman helped from in front, and Anita helped from behind, and when she was standing upright on the sidewalk,
she groped for Anita's arm and said, "Come upstairs with
me." That was terribly important.

"Of course."

Whoosh! the elevator went again, and she swallowed
carefully. At her door, Anita took the key and did the
unlocking, and they walked into a very familiar living room,
where Lavinia could sit down on the sofa and kick her shoes
off and close her eyes once more.

Anita didn't know what to do. She'd never seen Lavinia
drunk before, nor even imagined that such a thing was possible. And she had never before brought a drunken person
home or been responsible for somebody in that condition.

She couldn't just leave Lavinia there, half-sitting and
half-lying on the sofa, fully dressed except for her shoes. But
she didn't know what else she could possibly do.

In stories, people did one of two things in a situation
like this. Either they made a big pot of strong black coffee,
or they undressed the drunk and put him or her to bed.
Anita wasn't sure which was the proper thing in this instance, so she decided to do both.

She'd start the coffee first. She left Lavinia sleeping on
the sofa, and went in search of the kitchen.

It was a large and expensive-looking apartment. The living room was more than twice as large as Anita's, with a wall-to-wall green carpet, new-looking furniture, and a dark-wood bar in one corner. A broad-arched doorway led to the dining room, with gray carpeting wall-to-wall, a gleaming dark-wood table and chairs, and glass-fronted shelving which held polished crystal of all kinds. Beyond the dining room was the hall. A bathroom, all in green tile, was immediately to the right, and a bookshelf-lined den immediately to the left. Beyond the den, farther down the hall, she found the bedroom, done in pale blue and dominated by a huge double bed. Across the hall from the bedroom was the kitchen, a gleaming white laboratory-like room, with more shelf space than any one person could possibly need.

Lavinia apparently didn't believe in instant coffee. There was a percolator on the sideboard, and a can of coffee on one of the shelves. Anita started a whole potful, and went back to the living room.

Getting Lavinia to the bedroom looked as though it wasn't going to be easy. But she couldn't let her just lie there all night, in that awkward position and fully clothed. Anita remembered the few times she had slept all night with her clothes on, usually after being up late studying for a final, and she remembered how cottony she always felt the next morning.

Lavinia wasn't a particularly heavy woman, but neither was Anita a particularly strong girl. She simply couldn't carry the older woman to the bedroom. She'd have to get Lavinia awake enough to walk, that was all there was to it.

It wasn't readily done. Lavinia just didn't want to wake up. Anita pushed and prodded, reasoned and cajoled, and finally got Lavinia on her feet and in uncertain motion. They passed through the dining room, bumping against the table, through the hall and into the bedroom, where Lavinia sagged onto the bed with a relieved sigh, and went right back to sleep.

It was the first time Anita had ever undressed anyone but herself. Getting the stockings off was comparatively easy, but the dress and slip and undergarments took all her energy and ingenuity. The girdle was worst of all. But finally Lavinia's clothes were piled neatly on a chair, and Lavinia was lying on her back on the bed, nude and sleeping.

Anita next wrestled the covers out from underneath Lavinia, and was startled at the soft warmth of Lavinia's skin when she touched it. And Lavinia's body was surprisingly young, much younger than her face, flat-bellied and small-waisted. Even her breasts were much firmer than Anita would have thought possible in a woman Lavinia's age.

She suddenly realized she was standing with the sheet and blanket held up, halted in the motion of covering Lavinia, while she gazed at the older woman's body. She felt a hot flush of obscure embarrassment, and quickly lowered the covers into place. Then she heard the coffee perking hard across the hall.

She was grateful for the necessity to leave the bedroom. Hurrying to the kitchen, she unplugged the percolator and poured two cups of coffee. Bringing them back, she stopped in the doorway. Lavinia was wide awake and sitting up in bed, the covers fallen to her waist. They looked at one another.

"I made you coffee," Anita said. *Why do I feel so nervous?*

"You undressed me," Lavinia murmured softly. *Tonight? Tonight?*

Anita walked over to the bed and handed Lavinia her coffee. They still looked at one another.

"I didn't think you'd be waking up, so—so I undressed you." *I shouldn't be the first to look away. Why not?*

"Why did you make coffee for me, then?" *No, no, that's stupid! Don't rush her that way!*

"Sandra Keel came to me." *I wasn't going to tell her. Why? Why do I feel this way? Why?*

"Sit down here." Lavinia patted the bed. "You don't have to stand up."

Anita sat down, and that gave her the excuse to look away. She sipped at the coffee, which was too strong and too hot, and put it on the nightstand beside Lavinia's cup. Lavinia looked at her, and said, softly, "Why do you look so worried?"

"Sandra Keel came to me." *I wasn't going to tell her that!*

"She did?" *That bitch!* "When?"

"Last week. She—she's a lesbian." *Just like a pajama party, she'd said. But not with Sandra. If all lesbians were like Sandra . . . What do they do together? Why am I thinking about this? I ought to go home.*

"Did she make a pass at you?"

"Yes. She kissed me. She said you were a lesbian, too."

Lavinia was silent, and Anita turned hopeless eyes to her. "She said you were a lesbian, too." *What do I want her to answer? I ought to go home.*

"I heard you." *There's no reason to be afraid.*

Anita waited—they both waited—but Lavinia was silent. Finally, explosively, Anita whispered, "Are you?"

Lavinia nodded, carefully, watching the girl's face, clasping her hands together to keep them from shaking.

Anita looked away again. She couldn't meet the woman's eyes. "I wasn't sure."

"I am."

Anita swallowed, stared at the carpet, and the silence lengthened until she said, "What do you do?"

"Do?"

"What does a—what do you do, together?"

Lavinia felt her shoulder and back muscles tense, straining. "Do you really want to know?"

"Yes." Anita nodded convulsively.

"Come into bed with me."

Anita bit her lower lip, and they both waited again. Then she whispered, "I'm afraid."

"So am I."

Anita looked at her, and saw that Lavinia was afraid, too, and for some reason that made her own fear less. "Turn off the light," she whispered.

Lavinia reached out, the motion raising and firming her young-woman's breasts, and flicked off the lamp on the night table. The room was almost completely dark now, except for a vague, soft light filtering down the hall from the living room.

Anita slipped quickly out of her clothes, and Lavinia waited for her, unmoving, scarcely breathing, afraid that even now the girl might change her mind, might become too frightened and run away.

But Anita didn't run away. With a slight rustling of the sheets, she slipped into bed, and Lavinia reached out, her hand sliding around the warm, firm girl's skin to Anita's back, drawing her closer. Anita closed her eyes in the darkness and turned her face to Lavinia to be kissed.

Lavinia's lips were gentle against hers, Lavinia's hands warm on her body. Anita sighed, and opened her mouth for Lavinia's questing tongue.

Lavinia stroked the slender body of her new lover, and smiled against Anita's lips. "I'll show you what to do," she whispered.

They were no longer afraid, no longer unsure. They felt the hot excitement of touching and being touched, of kissing and being kissed, to loving and being loved. Anita felt a hot, tingling sensation go all through her and a sweet, aching warmth assailed her loins and she suddenly found herself cleaving frantically to Lavinia. And when their movements together slowed and stopped, they didn't know how much time had passed. The room was dark and warm and they lay silently together, wrapped in each other's arms.

It was so soothing at first, so comforting to be held close by Lavinia, but with silence and stillness came thought to Anita, and with thought came nervousness.

Now she knew. She had wanted to know, she had wanted to experience this, without admitting it to herself, and now she had done it. And now the filthy word applied to her, too.

She argued against the thought, and the nervousness. She wasn't filthy. The people at the party tonight had been filthy, and she wasn't like them. What she and Lavinia had done together could never be as evil as that.

She was still a virgin. So what had happened? She had come to this bed a virgin, and she was still a virgin, so nothing had happened.

It was almost like doing what that drunken man had accused her of doing at the party—almost like doing things alone. Was that so terribly wrong? Her teacher in Introductory Psychology had said that everybody did it, one time or another. It wasn't as wrong as going to bed with a man before you were married.

Lavinia whispered, "Stay here tonight," breaking into her thoughts. "Stay here tonight, and we'll get your things tomorrow."

"You want me to live here?"

"Of course." Lavinia kissed her again.

This time the mental struggle was stronger. Doing this with Lavinia once, out of curiosity, wasn't so very wrong. But to live here, to share a bed with Lavinia and do it every night, that was something else again. For instance she would have to lie to her parents about why she was moving. She would have to lie to everybody, hide from everybody.

But that didn't matter. That was only worrying about what people would think. Why should she care what people would think? All she cared about was how good it was to be lying here in the dark, cradled in Lavinia's arms. Nothing else mattered, she told herself determinedly, and this nervousness was downright silly. It would go away soon.

"I'm glad you want me to live with you," she whispered, and snuggled closer against Lavinia, waiting for the nervousness to go away.

6

MONDAY MORNING, nine-twenty, and the elevator doors slid open. Lavinia Cartwright marched through the steno pool, Anita trailing in her wake. They went down the long hall together, and Lavinia paused before the door of Anita's office. She patted Anita's forearm, smiled, and said, "See you at lunchtime, honey."

"All right," said Anita, and managed a smile of her own. She kept the smile alive as she exchanged good mornings with Mrs. Marshall, but let it die naturally the minute she was in the privacy of her own office.

She could be alone now, until one o'clock. She had no appointments this morning, no one to see until three o'clock this afternoon. She didn't have to force a smile for another three and a half hours, didn't have to fight to keep from trembling, didn't have to work so very hard to hide her nervousness.

Three weeks now she'd been living with Lavinia, sleeping with Lavinia, making love with Lavinia, and the nervousness hadn't gone away. Instead it had grown worse, and she was afraid to let anyone see it. Afraid to let Lavinia see it, because she couldn't answer Lavinia's questions—she couldn't risk losing Lavinia. She did love Lavinia, did need her, did want to live with her.

But how could she answer the questions of anyone else in the world? "I'm nervous because I'm a lesbian."

She had to talk to somebody. She'd been bottling it up for three weeks now, and it was tearing at her, the nervousness was getting worse and worse. She absolutely had to talk to somebody about it—talk it out of her system or go crazy.

But she had no one to talk to. Not her old roommate, not Mrs. Marshall, not any of the girls at work. Not any *woman*—she could never tell a woman about this.

She hung her coat up and sat down behind her desk. The morning mail was stacked neatly in the middle of the desk blotter. She picked up the first letter and started to read. She forced herself to concentrate on the letter, and the tumbling thoughts and doubts and fears receded into the background of her mind.

Barry blinked steadily and solemnly at the typewriter. He had typed three words, in the last two hours. "Lots of men . . ." He could think of plenty of words to finish that sentence, but none of them were printable. And whatever thought had originally been in his head when he'd started the sentence was gone forever.

"Why I ever try to work on a Monday," he told the typewriter solemnly, "I will never know." He double-spaced and typed, in capital letters, "WEEKENDS SHOULD BE

ABOLISHED." He studied that for a minute, double-spaced again, and typed, "Dorothy, come home. All is forgiven."

He growled in self-disgust, ripped the sheet from the typewriter, crumpled it and hurled it at the wastebasket.

Why in the name of God couldn't he forget Dorothy? This Grand Passion bit was a bore and a time-waster and a terrible strain on the nerves. Not to mention the loins. He hadn't been near a woman since Dorothy had gone west for her divorce, four months ago.

Why not? He knew damn well why not. Because he was scared out of his mind. He'd been burned, but good, and he wasn't about to play with fire soon again.

There was also the little problem that he still wanted Dorothy. She had given him a couple of years of fire and brimstone, of the kind of marriage that drove men to monasteries. Yet he still wanted her back. If *Time* magazine knew about this, he told himself, they'd make me Boob Of The Year.

He looked at his watch. The big hand was on the six and the little hand was on the four, and after a while he figured it out. Four-thirty. And he was still hung-over.

The pill bottles stood smugly in a row on his otherwise denuded desk top. The typewriter, on its own stand to his right, gave him the look reserved for slackers and ne'er-do-wells. He thought he just might as well go home now, rather than wait till five o'clock.

And here she came again, bursting into the office, Anita Rawlins, girl wonder. "Can I talk to you for a minute, Barry?" she begged. Her voice was unnaturally high-pitched, and her hands were clasping and fidgeting together. She was so upset she could hardly stand still.

"What's wrong?" he asked her. He rose from the chair, wondering what in the world could have shaken her up so much.

"I've got to talk to somebody," she said, rushing the words, still talking in that high-pitched voice. "I can't talk about it to a girl. And you're the only man I know—the only one I could talk to."

"Hey, take it easy," he said. He came around and took her hands, leading her to the leather-covered chair beside his desk. Her hands were quaking and trembling as he held them, and she was staring at him as though the orphanage had just burned down. "Sit down," he said. "Take it easy. Relax a minute."

She sat, stiff and unrelaxed, and he went back to his own seat, and said, "What is it, Anita? What happened?"

"I don't know how to say it," she said, and he could see she was on the verge of tears.

"Just say it, then," he suggested. "What happened?"

"I—I'm living with Lavinia." This was said so fast he could barely understand it, and then she was silent, as though that explained everything.

"Yes?" he prompted her. "So what?"

"I'm *living* with her." She looked away, fidgeting nervously, blinking back the tears, then looked back to say, all in a rush, "I'm *sleeping* with her, don't you see? With Lavinia. We go to bed together."

"You—" He stopped, his mouth open. Did she mean what he thought she meant? She couldn't. "You mean she's a dyke? Uh, homosexual, I mean."

She nodded spastically, and the eyes overflowed. She hunched forward, her hands pressed against her face, her shoulders trembling, the sound of her weeping muffled by her hands. "For three weeks," she said, gasping between sobs, the words just barely intelligible. "I had to talk to somebody. I've been going crazy, I've been so nervous. I don't know what to do." She raised her face suddenly, red-blotched and tear-streaked, aching-eyed.

"Well, uh—" He was lost, completely out of his depth. What was he supposed to say? "You, uh—well, what do you *want* to do?"

"I don't know!" And the tears came harder. "I don't know, I'm afraid. I can't stand it any more—"

"Listen," he said. "Look now." He got to his feet, reaching for her elbow, and lifted her up from the chair. The girl was in no shape to talk or listen, too nervous to know which way was up. And Barry knew only one sure cure for a state like that. "You need a drink," he said. "Come on, it's late enough."

"I can't—let people—see me this way," she wailed. Her breathing was labored, and the words were torn out of her in little bursts.

"Wait here," he said. "I'll get your coat."

He hurried through the offices, got Anita's coat and hurried back. She was still crying, but less rackingly. He helped her into her coat, telling her not to worry as she kept saying that she couldn't let anybody see her looking this way. "There's another way out of here," he told her. "Come on."

They went out to the executive stairway, and down one flight to the eighteenth floor. A door took them directly to the main hall on that floor, and they met no one as they walked to the elevator. Barry held Anita's arm, and glanced worriedly at her as they walked. It had all been too fast to absorb. Lavinia being a dyke, for one thing. Why, the grape-vine had it that Lavinia and Jake had once had an affair. And less than a year ago, the same grapevine had it, Lavinia had been living with that crummy photographer, Greg some-body-or-other. When the hell had she changed teams? And why?

And this Anita. Lavinia going butch was tough enough to believe, but Anita being her playmate was too crazy. If anybody else in the world had told him Anita was sleeping with Lavinia, he wouldn't have accepted it for a second. Yet Anita herself had told him, and now he didn't know what to believe.

But he knew what to do. He had had experience with nervous tension. "You'll be okay," he told her. "A drink or two to calm you down, that's what you need."

She nodded, miserable and shaken, but no longer crying. "All right," she said.

The waiter stopped at the table and said, "Last call, folks. We close at two."

Anita looked at her watch. "It's ten minutes to two! I thought it wasn't even eleven o'clock yet."

"Better make the last round doubles," Barry told the waiter. When the man had gone, he grinned at Anita and said, "Is it really that late? We've got to get to work in the morning."

"Where did the time go? I thought we just barely got here."

They had started at a place on Fifth Avenue, couple of blocks from the office. After two drinks there, Anita had calmed down somewhat, enough to realize how relieved she was that she had finally told someone, and to realize also just how beautifully Barry had responded. He hadn't asked her a million questions. He hadn't turned away from her in disgust. He had merely waited, talking calmly with her, soothing her, letting her tell the story her own way and at her own speed.

She had told him everything. First at the bar, and then at the restaurant where they went for dinner, she had told him the whole story, about Sandra and Lavinia and the situation she was now in. He had listened soberly, and he had offered no glib advice.

"I don't know what you should do," he had told her. "If living with Lavinia makes you this nervous, then maybe you shouldn't live with her. But if you want to live with her, no matter what, then the only thing you can do is accept it and quit worrying about it. If you can't do that, I don't know what to tell you. I can't make any moral judgments for you. I'm the last guy in the world who could do that. It's strictly up to you, whatever you really want for yourself."

Then slowly the subject had changed, and they had talked about other things. After the restaurant, they had come here, and spent a long time with each drink, just talking. They had told each other their life stories. They had talked about anything and everything. Now the nervousness was completely gone, and she felt relaxed and happy, and warmly grateful to Barry for having done this for her.

But now they had to leave, the night was ending. Waiters were taking the tablecloths off the empty tables. They were practically the only ones left in the place. The evening was coming to an end, and she didn't want it to end. Where could she go? Only back with Lavinia, and she didn't want to do that. Not now, not yet. That meant making the decision, and she didn't want to have to make the decision—not quite yet.

They walked out to the sidewalk, and the night air was crisp and clear. "I don't want to go home yet," she said.

"What about coming to my place?" he asked her. "We could have a nightcap, and gab some more. That's all, I promise. I'm still gun-shy so I won't be making any passes."

"I'd like to," she said, and he waved at an empty cab.

They sat close, but not touching, in the cab. Barry lived on West Seventy-seventh Street, near the park, and his apartment was somewhere between Lavinia's place and Anita's old apartment on Forty-sixth Street. There was an elevator, and the apartment was clean, but it was smaller than Lavinia's, and the furniture didn't look quite as new.

Anita sat on the davenport, while Barry mixed drinks. He came over, handed Anita her drink, and said, "To pleasant evenings that rush by too fast."

"Yes," she said, smiling at him, and they clinked glasses.

They were silent for a few seconds, and then he said, not looking at her, "Where will you go, after you leave here?"

There it was again. She shook her head, not wanting to think about it, feeling the beginnings of the nervousness again. "I don't know."

"Do you have any place to stay? If you decide not to go back to Lavinia's, I mean."

"I—I'm not sure. I still have a key to my old place. My roommate isn't in town, but she may have found somebody else to move in there by now. Maybe I could go there."

"Do you want to?"

"I don't want to think about it yet."

This time the tears took her by surprise. She hadn't known she was going to cry, but all of a sudden it welled up inside her, and she was weeping. "Hey, come on," he said, and pulled her close to him. She pressed her face against his chest. "Come on," he whispered. "Take it easy. You don't have to decide yet. You don't have to go anywhere yet."

He held her, and she pressed tight to him, knowing the relief of unashamed weeping. And his arms were so strong around her, so different from Lavinia's arms—the smell of him, the touch of him was so different.

They were a man's arms and a man's chest, and a man's voice husky in her ears, and she knew this was the way it was supposed to be—this was right, this was the only way the sickly touch of woman could be wiped from her body.

"Barry," she whispered. "Barry, I don't want to go home."

His arms tightened around her, and when she raised her face, he kissed her, and his hands were fumbling with her clothes, and then he was carrying her to the bedroom. As if in a dream, she let him strip away her dress and under-things, saw him throw off his own clothes.

Different, different, it was all so different. His hands were stronger, more demanding, as they stroked her body, his lips were more firm, more insistent. He kissed her gently at first, but her own ardor spurred him on. His tongue pierced her mouth and their lips ground and writhed against each other. Anita felt a warm heaviness in her loins and there was a burgeoning fullness in her breasts, the nipples growing taut and firm. Then his hands were stroking her there and his lips slid from her mouth to her throat and then to her breasts and the swelling ardor of her feelings made her arch her body wantonly against him.

Oddly enough, she didn't want the light off with Barry. She wanted to see him, she wanted to know the difference, she wanted the sight and touch and desire of him to wash away the guilty echo of Lavinia.

The pain was sudden, sharp, tearing, and suddenly gone, and a delirious sensation poured through her—sharp and electric and almost unbearably good. She and Barry were one—moving together, and *this* was the art and the act of love, and the rest had all been only shadow.

With Lavinia, their love-making had always ended slowly, descending from excitement to silence and soothing comfort. But this was stronger, building and growing until there couldn't be any more.

And then the world exploded. Rigid, tense, straining, clasped together, the silence roared, exploded, going out and out, and she screamed through the roaring silence and clawed at his back, sinking her teeth into his shoulder.

She was so weak. He was lying beside her now, his forearm across his face to shield his eyes from the light. She touched him hesitantly, in awe, and smiled, and was too weak to move or talk.

Slowly, she came down from the peak, moving reluctantly back to reality. There was a pressure inside her body now that hadn't been there before. She knew what it was, and she knew that this time it had happened.

This was completion, this was reality, and beside this the fumbling of Lavinia was the touch of a ghost. This was completion.

But wrong! This was the evil thing! This was the act against which she'd been warned all her life. Not the fumbling with Lavinia. That was nothing, really. This was sinning. She was no longer a virgin.

The tears this time were less clearly motivated. They were for everything. Tears of relief, from the tearing climax of love. Tears of loss, for she was no longer virginal. Tears of pain, because she had committed the most terrible sin.

Weeping, she turned to Barry, to hide against him, to be consoled and protected and loved. At her touch, he rolled away and got to his feet. He stood with his back to her, his shoulders hunched, and she stared up at him, not understanding. "Barry?" she whispered.

He didn't turn to face her. "You can't stay here all night, you know," he said.

Why the hell had he let it happen? He stood glaring at the wall, afraid to look at her, and listened to the echo of his words. He knew they were cruel, but he couldn't help it. He couldn't let her build anything from this. He had to cut it off right here.

How had he gotten into this? He hadn't even seen it coming. He'd invited her up here to the apartment, sure, but he hadn't figured on this. She was half-lesbian and half-idiot. Who would have expected her all of a sudden to hop into bed with him? Nobody, that's who.

Tears, tears, tears! The girl wept gallons of them. A regular Old Faithful. Every quarter-hour, like clockwork, the floodgates opened, and she was off again, crying her neurotic little heart out.

That's what had done it in the first place. Weeping all over his office, so he'd felt sorry for her. Then taking her out for a drink and letting her bend his ear for hour after hour, until she conned him into inviting her up here. Then going weepy all over again, so that he had to play big brother, give her a nice strong shoulder to cry on, pat her little head for her.

And all at once, he had known she wanted it. He didn't know where the knowledge had come from, or how, but he had felt it as an urgent certainty.

And it had been so goddamn long since he'd had a woman that he hadn't had sense enough to throw her out of the apartment before anything could happen. Oh, no, not him! *He* had to carry her off to the bedroom.

He knew how to take it from there. He knew what the program was now. His role was to rescue her from the nasty old dyke. Her next move would be to move in here with him, and they'd run around the apartment naked all the time, pinching each other and giggling, and she'd forget all about that lesbian nonsense and from now on want it the good old American way. Until pretty soon they'd decide to make it legal, and go get married—and live miserably ever after.

No thanks! He'd been through that last act once already, and once was more than enough. Better to hurt her a little bit, all at once, right now, ending it forever, than to let it drag on for months or years, with both of them being hurt a hell of a lot and steadily.

"Barry," she whispered again, and the pleading in the word, the naked begging of it, grated on him. The girl had no self-respect, no pride, nothing. She didn't want a bed-mate, she wanted a parent. Barry or Lavinia, it didn't matter which. And maybe she'd like both, so she could have both a Mama and a Papa. Sleep with Mama on Tuesday, Thursday and Saturday, with Papa on Monday, Wednesday and Friday. On Sunday, all three of them would crawl into one great big bed, and go out of their loving minds.

Barry knew he was being unfair to the girl, but he didn't care. He wanted to be unfair to her. He wanted to get mad at her. He wanted to make it possible to throw her out for good and all, to make it impossible to weaken and crawl back into bed with her and kiss her and hold her and tell her she could stay all night or all year or forever if she wanted.

"I'm not your salvation," he said, but he still didn't dare turn around. "I'm not the right guy. Go find somebody your own age and experience. Go find somebody who's more your type."

"Barry, please—"

"And quit that sniffling."

He was shocked himself at the vehemence of it. In embarrassed confusion, he fled to the kitchen. He kept himself busy, brewing a pot of coffee, until after a while he heard her footsteps, and the hall door opened and closed, and she was gone.

He should have felt relieved. Damn it, he should have felt relieved.

It was almost four o'clock, and Lavinia was waiting up for her, sitting in the semi-dark living room. Anita let herself into the apartment, trying to be silent, expecting Lavinia to be in bed and asleep, and stopped dead when she saw Lavinia sitting there.

"I was afraid you weren't coming back," said Lavinia, and her voice was soft, her face expressionless. "I was afraid you'd left me."

Anita shook her head. "I—I was nervous. I had to be away for a little while, be by myself . . ." She wanted to tell Lavinia about Barry, about what had happened tonight, but she couldn't. Lavinia would hate her. Lavinia wouldn't have anything more to do with her if she ever found out what had happened tonight, how filthy Anita had been and what a fool she had made of herself.

The memory of Barry cut her like a knife. She had been a fool. She had trusted him, she had told him everything, given herself to him, done with him that final thing she had never done before with any man. And he had been brutal. He had ordered her out—refused to even look at her. She understood then that he had only been using her, as a man does a woman, and that his kindness and his concern had been nothing but a mask.

"You don't have to tell me about it if you don't want to," Lavinia said. "Where you've been, I mean. It doesn't matter, since you've come back."

She was so ashamed. Lavinia was good and kind and gentle. Lavinia loved her. Lavinia would never use her. And tonight she had betrayed Lavinia. She could never tell her about it, she could never confess it, and she was grateful that Lavinia wasn't going to question her.

Lavinia got to her feet, in one smooth, easy motion, and held out her hand. "We'd better go to bed," she said. "We have to get up early in the morning."

"Yes." Anita took the outstretched hand, and they walked together into the bedroom. They undressed quickly,

and Anita was terrified that there would be something different about her body now, something that would show, that
somehow Lavinia would be able to tell what had occurred. It
seemed impossible that she could look the same, that there
could be no mark on her at all.

They got into bed, and Lavinia switched off the light,
then held out her arms, and Anita came into their protection.
Lavinia stroked her hair, kissed her cheek, and murmured,
"Don't leave me, Anita. Don't ever leave me."

Anita shivered, and pressed closer to the other woman.
"I won't leave you," she whispered. "I couldn't ever leave
you."

7

BARRY PROWLED HIS OFFICE like a caged wolf, glaring at the walls and the window, from time to time kicking at pieces of furniture, growling in his throat every time his thoughts completed their closed circle and brought back the haunting face of Anita Rawlins.

For three days he'd successfully avoided both Anita and Lavinia completely. During that time he hadn't seen Anita once, but her face was as clear and as large in his mind as though she'd just this minute stepped out of the room.

It was stupid. Yesterday afternoon, he had spent three hours sitting at the typewriter, trying to get something done on the page and a half for next month's *Milady,* and he hadn't been able to concentrate worth a damn. Three hours at the typewriter, and the result was now lying on his desk. It was a single sheet of typing paper, and on it he had written, "Thinking about Anita Rawlins is: (1) Ridiculous, because I'm fifteen years older than she is. (2) Absurd, because she's a lesbian and she's living with Lavinia Cartwright.

(3) Useless, because I pretty effectively got rid of her Monday night. (4) Dangerous, because it could conceivably lead to marriage, and I don't want to go through that again. (5) Impossible to avoid."

Number five was the snapper. It was impossible to avoid thinking about Anita. Barry knew it because he'd been trying for three days now to think about something else.

The page and a half, for instance. Here it was Thursday, and the deadline for the next issue was Friday, and he hadn't yet turned out one word of copy.

He continued to prowl the office, glaring and growling and kicking. Finally he sat down at the typewriter again. He slipped a fresh sheet of paper into the machine, poised his hands over the keys, and waited. And waited. And growled again, disgusted with himself.

He was acting like a high school kid, for God's sake. He was a romantic at heart, a sucker from the word go. For months, he'd been going around mooning about Dorothy, even though he knew full well that the worst possible thing that could happen to him would be to have Dorothy back. But still he'd mooned. Now, at last, Dorothy was out of his head. And what had done the trick? He'd found somebody else to moon over.

"Barry, boy," he growled at himself, "you are the world's dopiest adolescent."

All at once, he began to type furiously. "My feelings toward Anita are: (1) Protective. I want to help her, get her out of this lesbian thing before it's too late. (2) Erotic. Because I took her to bed with me, and I'd like to do it again. (3) Passionate. I'm in love with her. (4) All of the above."

He read what he'd written, grimaced, and double-spaced then typed again. "I am: (1) adolescent. (2) A dope. (3) A jerk. (4) All of the above."

A deadline coming up tomorrow, and what was he doing? Multiple-choice questions about Anita, for God's sake.

Maybe he could do a multiple-choice quiz for the magazine, come to think of it. Kill a half a page that way. There now, he was thinking about work for a change. Wasn't that peaches and cream?

Multiple choice. On what subject? Coal-mining in New South Wales. Baseball pitchers of yesteryear. Swipe the photo-quiz gimmick from *Look,* maybe.

Sure. And take a flying leap out the window, maybe.

The thing was, he wanted Anita. That was the whole point—he *wanted* her. He didn't care if he was fifteen years older than she. He didn't care if she was as dyke as a lady wrestler. He didn't care if the whole thing would wind up the way it had with Dorothy. He just wanted Anita, period.

So there he was, full circle again. Time after time, in the last three days, he had come to that admission, and started right off with the doubts and the worries and the reasons-why-not again, only to circle all the way around and come back to the indisputable fact that he wanted Anita.

Enough. He was going to get some work done. He was going to ignore the whole thing. He'd fill that page and a half lickety-split, he would.

Now, what the hell do you put in hubby's page and a half of *Milady*? He couldn't think of anything that could possibly belong there. He couldn't think of anything, let's face it, except Anita.

Enough! He pounded the desk, jumped to his feet, looked determined, and stalked across the room to the table where back issues of *Milady* were stacked. He would see what kind of thing he'd done in the past for that page and a half, and maybe that would give him some ideas.

He stood at the table, one hand touching the stack of magazines, and said aloud, "Anita, will you come home with me tonight? Will you come home with me and stay with me?"

He sighed, and the fight went out of him. All right. He'd ask her. He'd tell her he was sorry for the way he'd acted Monday night, and he'd ask her to come home with him tonight. All right. Then maybe he could get some work done.

The decision made, he was suddenly apprehensive. He'd been pretty rotten Monday night, after all. What if she turned him down? What if she'd gone back to Lavinia, for good?

"I can *ask* her," he reminded himself. The least she could do was say no. So what was there to get so upset about? He thought he must be a case of arrested development. He'd never stopped being a high school sophomore.

It was time for action. Over the top, tallyho, full speed ahead. And try not to look so grim, you clown, you'll scare her half to death.

He left his office and marched across the hall. To Mrs. Marshall, typing steadily at her desk, he said, "Anita in?"

"Yes. Shall I tell her—"

"Never mind, I'll just barge on in. Uh, is she talking with somebody?"

"No, she isn't."

"Thanks."

She was sitting behind the huge and cluttered desk, looking absurdly young for this office. She glanced up at him with surprise that changed rapidly to cold impersonality. "Yes?" she said.

"Anita, I—" He faltered, tried again. "Listen, I just wanted to tell you I was sorry."

She raised one eyebrow, and he knew she was imitating Lavinia. "Sorry?" she echoed, as though she didn't know what he was talking about. She was imitating Lavinia there, too, but he didn't care.

"About Monday night. I was—well, you know I was married once, and it turned out rotten, and—"

"You don't have to explain anything, Barry," she said. She was being very cold and very impersonal. "We'd both had too much to drink, that was all. I'm sure we won't let it happen again."

"We hadn't had too much to drink. Neither of us. Listen, I don't blame you for being mad at me—"

"I'm not mad at you, Barry. It was as much my fault as it was yours."

He gestured helplessly, stymied by her coldness. "I just—I just wanted to tell you I was sorry, and—well, and that I *do* want it to happen again. Only the aftermath would be different." He'd started now, and he rushed on before she could interrupt. "I told you I was gun-shy, I told you about my marriage. That was what did it. I was afraid to get involved, you see? So I was rotten to you because I didn't want to give anything a chance to happen. But I was wrong. Anita, listen, can we start all over again? Blank sheet, right from the top. All right?"

"I'm afraid not, Barry," she said, and her words were still icy. "I don't think we'd do well together at all."

"Anita, listen—" They were on the tip of his tongue— the words he was afraid to say, because they made it too definite, too final—but now he forced them out, because it was the only way. "I love you, Anita," he said. "That's the truth, and I've been over there in my office trying to deny it for the last three days. I'm in love with you."

She shook her head. "I don't think you are, Barry," she said. "I think you're just embarrassed over Monday night, and you're dramatizing it."

That rocked him. She was sitting there, wrapped in ice, cutting him down as though he practically didn't exist. The Anita of Monday, the Anita of today—what had made this change, what had changed her so completely in only three days?

There was only one thing that could have done it. "Are you back with Lavinia?" he asked her.

"Yes, I am." It was said as impersonally as the rest, with no embarrassment and no nervousness. "I took your advice. I accepted things the way they were, and stopped worrying."

"Anita, listen—"

"I'm back with Lavinia permanently." She looked away from him, calmly, and picked up a sheet of paper from her desk. "I'm rather busy right now, Barry, what with the deadline coming up tomorrow and everything."

"Anita, life with Lavinia—"

"Don't talk against Lavinia." She glared at him now. "It won't do you any good."

He made vague hand motions, feeling as though there must be something more he could say, some way to convince her.

But she was ignoring him now, copy-editing a manuscript, and he knew he'd been dismissed, and that there was nothing at all left for him to say.

Not to Anita. But there was plenty he could say to Lavinia.

Would that do any good? He could go to Lavinia, demand that she leave Anita alone, threaten her with exposure, force her to give Anita up. With Anita on her own again, away from the influence of Lavinia, he might have a chance. He *would* have a chance.

He turned away from Anita, who continued to ignore him, and hurried from the office. He went back to his own office, through the door to the executive stairway, and walked directly into Lavinia's office.

Lavinia was standing at the work table across the room, talking with an illustrator, motioning at a drawing on the table. She looked around when she heard the door open and said, "Barry. Hello. What brings you here?"

"I'd like to talk to you in private, Lavinia."

The illustrator, taking the hint, said a last few words to Lavinia, picked up the drawing, and left the room. Lavinia crossed to her desk, picked up a pack of cigarettes, and said, "What is it? You look deadly serious. Going to miss the deadline?"

"It's about Anita," he said.

Her reaction was almost too small to be seen. She paused for just a second in the lighting of her cigarette, tensed for that second, and then completed the motion.

"Anita? What about her?"

"I want you to give her up."

Lavinia's look of puzzlement was almost good enough to be real. "Give her up? But she's doing very good work. There hasn't been a single complaint—"

"You know what I'm talking about."

The bewildered smile was perfect. "No, I don't, Barry."

"Then I'll spell it out for you. You and Anita have been living together—"

"Rooming together," Lavinia corrected softly. "Sharing an apartment."

"*Living* together. Sleeping together. And I want you—"

"*What?*" Lavinia's shock was even better than the real thing. She seemed totally nonplused. "Barry, are you suggesting—"

"I'm not suggesting a damn thing. I'm telling you. You and Anita have been having a lesbian affair, and—"

"That's a damned lie!"

Barry felt one second of serious doubt. Lavinia was glaring at him, shocked and outraged, high circles of color on her cheeks, the very picture of indignant truth. For one second, he wondered if Anita had been lying. Some dream fantasy of her own, some neurotic impulse . . . But the second passed, and he knew that Anita had been telling the truth, and that Lavinia's denial was false. "It isn't a lie," he said. "You've turned lesbian, and you've dragged Anita down with you."

"I don't know who's been spreading such malicious—"

"If you're wondering who told me," he interrupted, "I'll tell you. Anita."

The shock this time was real. Barry could see the difference—between the false shock of before and this true shock now. Lavinia moved her lips without speaking, turned away, looked back, finally said, her voice barely above a whisper, "She wouldn't. She wouldn't say such a thing."

"She did. She was with me Monday night—"

"She wouldn't say such a thing!" Lavinia was back in control of herself now, and blazing at him. She turned away, heading for the connecting door between this room and Anita's office. "We'll just get her in here and find out—"

"Don't do it, Lavinia." He didn't want Anita in here now. That would kill the whole thing. She'd never forgive him for having gone to Lavinia. "Don't do it," he repeated. "I'm warning you, Lavinia."

She stopped, her hand on the doorknob, looked back at him. "Warning me? Warning me about what?"

"You're going to sit down and listen to me," he said. "You're not going to drag Anita in here, to try to intimidate her. You're going to listen to what I have to say."

"Why am I?"

"Because otherwise I go upstairs and talk to Jake."

"And repeat that ridiculous accusation?"

"And repeat that true accusation. Right."

She released the doorknob, and walked back to him, smiling with self-assurance. "Go right ahead," she said. "Go right on up and tell him, if you want to. And he'll laugh in your face. Jake and I—"

"I know all about Jake and you," he snapped. "That was twenty years ago. It doesn't mean a thing for today, and Jake will know it. Jake married but you never did. When I explain that you fired Sandra Keel as a result of a lovers' quarrel—"

"Sandra Keel! Barry, have you been drinking? The next thing you'll do is claim every girl working here is lesbian."

"Not every girl. Just you. Just you and Sandra, and she isn't here any more." He shook a threatening finger at her. "Not Anita. That girl is straight, she isn't a dyke. She—"

"Don't use that word. I hate it."

"I imagine you do."

Lavinia ignored the remark. She crossed to her desk and stubbed out her cigarette, then turned to say, "I thought Anita was supposed to be my lover. Now you say she isn't a lesbian."

"Not yet she isn't. But you're well on the way to turning her into one."

Lavinia's smile was mocking. "And I haven't succeeded yet? I must be slipping."

"No, you haven't succeeded yet. She hasn't followed your path all the way yet."

"Barry, I'm trying to keep my temper. You've come in here—"

"I have something to say to you, about Anita."

Lavinia held one hand up for silence. "Please. Let me say only this one thing. You have come into my office, accusing me of a terrible perversion, threatening to spread this lie all over, shouting at me, accusing me of leading Anita Rawlins astray, as though I were some melodramatic white slaver, and—I don't know what all. Now, I know you've been upset the last few months, since your wife left you—"

"My wife doesn't have a thing to do with this."

"Please. Just let me finish. I know you've been upset lately. I know you have had personal problems. Your work has grown more and more slipshod. I myself have covered for you more than once—"

"The point is—"

"The *point* is," she said, overriding him, "that I have done my best to keep my temper, knowing the strain you have been under the last few months. But I'm not sure I can keep it much longer. If you want to keep on working here—"

"All right," he said. "That's enough. I've listened to you, now you're going to listen to me."

"If you'll try not to interrupt—"

He reached her in two quick strides, grabbed her by the upper arms, and half-carried her across the room to the sofa, where he pushed her to a sitting position and stood glaring down at her, fists clenched at his sides. "You're going to listen to me," he said, "if I have to tape your mouth shut."

"This is intolerable!" She moved as though to get up, but he shoved her back, not gently, and this time she stayed where she was, staring wide-eyed up at him.

"Now," he said breathlessly. "You and Anita have been sleeping together for almost a month. You—"

"We have not!"

"Shut up!" He grabbed her shoulders and shook her, violently, and her head snapped back and forth like a hysterical metronome. "Shut up," he said again. "One more word, and I swear to God I tape your mouth shut."

She cringed back on the sofa, staring up at him, not speaking.

"All right," he said. "Now, you and Anita have been sleeping together. You are lesbian, one hundred percent. Anita isn't, but she's headed that way, and the only way to stop it is for you to stay away from her. Therefore, you will tell her this afternoon that the whole thing is off between you, and that she has to move out of your apartment. Right away. If you don't, I *will* spread the story everywhere, and I'll start with Jake."

He was finished. He'd said what he'd come to say, and he backed away from her and stood panting in the middle of the room, fumbling in his shirt pocket for his cigarettes.

She had been afraid of him, when he was leaning over her, shouting at her, but now he saw the fear lessen and gradually disappear. He watched Lavinia growing calm and once more assured, until finally she said, "In the first place, Barry, I deny your accusation. I deny it vehemently."

"Deny it all you want," he said. "But Anita moves out of your place today, or I go to Jake. You stay away from Anita from now on, or I go to Jake."

"Let me get something straight," she said. "You say that *I* am homosexual because I've been sleeping with Anita. Then you say that Anita *isn't* homosexual even though she's been sleeping with me. Now, that just doesn't make any sense, Barry. Nor does it make any sense that Anita, if she were sleeping with me, which she isn't, would go to you and tell you about it."

"She came to me because she was confused and upset and unhappy, and wanted somebody to talk to. Because she knew she was at the point where she had to decide, for good and all, whether she was going to turn lesbian or not."

Lavinia shook her head. "I'm sorry, Barry, it's too fantastic. If Anita is supposedly sleeping with me, then Anita must be a lesbian. And if Anita is a lesbian, I don't see what your interest in her is at all."

"Anita was in my bed Monday night," he told her softly. "That's why I know she isn't homosexual yet."

Lavinia's reaction to that was immediate—a cold, furious glare of utter hatred. "Anita went to bed with you?"

"Is that jealousy I see?" he asked her, feeling for the first time in the interview that he had the upper hand. "Yes, Anita went to bed with me."

But Lavinia had the ability to recover fast. Before he was finished speaking, her face was bland and blank again, and a contemptuous smile was forming at the corners of her lips. "Is that your test for heterosexuality, Barry? The fact that Anita would go to bed with you?"

"It seems like a pretty good test."

"Does it? Very well, then." She got up from the sofa and walked over to the door leading to the outer office. A button in the doorknob, when pressed, locked the door to anyone outside. Lavinia pressed this button now, and turned back to Barry. "I deny your accusation," she said. "I deny every part of it. Now, why don't you test me the way you tested Anita?"

He hadn't expected this. Whatever reaction he had thought to get from her, he had certainly never expected this. "Don't be silly," he said. "That isn't the point at all."

"Of course, it is. You say I'm a lesbian. I say I'm not. You've told me the terms of your test, and I say I'm willing to meet them."

"It isn't a test," he said, wondering how he'd become entangled in the bizarre situation. "I never said anything about a test."

While he'd been talking, she had hiked her skirt up and was now pulling off her girdle, panties and stockings. "You made the wrong accusation, Barry," she said, smiling bitterly at him. "Didn't Jack Alexander tell you about me, when you took over his job?" She tossed the underclothes onto the floor and shrugged her skirt back down into place. "When he used to work here," she said, "I'd take those things off every morning, as soon as I got to work. When Jack wanted sex, he wanted it right away. He used to come in here, and all he'd say was, 'Down and at it, Lavinia.' And he'd throw me down on that sofa there. We didn't even take time to take our clothes off."

"I don't care what you did five years ago," he said, trying desperately to get the conversation back where it belonged. "All I care about is Anita."

"You want her? She's yours. I say I'm not a lesbian, and I say I'm willing to prove it." She put her hands on her hips and stood spread-legged, grinning at him. "What's the matter, Barry? Wouldn't *you* pass the test?"

"There isn't any test," he insisted. "You're running away from the point."

"I'm not the one running away, Barry, you are. You've got homosexuality on the mind. Maybe *you're* the one who ought to be accused."

He gaped at her, not believing it. "Me? There's never been the slightest—"

"What are you doing working for a magazine like *Milady?* What are you doing wildly accusing other people of homosexuality? And why do you look so terrified when I show you my legs?" She rolled her hips, slowly, tauntingly. "Here it is, Barry girl," she said, mocking him. "Here it is. If you're a man, you want it."

"All I want is for you to stay away from Anita!"

She took a slow step toward him, still rolling her hips, her eyes glinting at him. "I'm a lesbian, am I, Barry? Why don't you find out for yourself? You're so sure of yourself, why don't you prove it? Aren't you man enough?"

"Damn you," he whispered. His fists were clenched again, and he glared at her, hating her for turning the tables on him this way. He wanted to beat her, to lash out at her, conquer her, force her to submit.

"Come and get it," she murmured. "If you know how."

Roaring with rage, he leaped at her, grabbing her with harsh, cruelly gripping hands, pulling her against him, kissing her savagely, forcing her backward and down. The sofa was too far away, so he pushed her backward and they crashed together to the floor.

He fumbled with his clothing, pushed her skirt up to her waist, and she was slapping at him, clawing him with raking fingernails, whispering harshly, "Can you, damn you, can you? I'll show you I'm not!"

Then he was ready and coming to her, and all at once she went rigid, her eyes widening with fear, and she cried, "No! Don't, don't!"

She twisted, rolling away, trying to get free of him, but he grabbed a handful of hair and yanked her back, twisting the hair, and fell on her, his mouth brutal on hers, choking down her scream.

She fought him like a wild woman, kicking and biting and scratching, trying to roll him away from her, but he clung, driving, strong in his victory, conquering her. His lips were stretched in a taut grin and he whispered, "Can you, Lavinia? Can you? You filthy dyke, you won't get away, and you can't pass the test, can you?"

"Stop!" she shrieked. "Get away from me!" But he bit down on her mouth again, ending her crying out, and drove on, exultant in his victory—until it was finished, and he was crawling to his feet, and she lay curled on the floor on her side, knees pulled up against her chest, the skirt still hiked high. She lay gasping, her quivering hands clasping one another, her eyes staring up at him with terror and revulsion.

"You couldn't, could you?" he said, glaring at her in triumph. Shakily, he lit himself a cigarette and paced around the office, unable to keep still, nerves still stretched taut. "You thought you could still go back, but you couldn't. You've crossed the line, haven't you?"

"I've loved men," she whispered, as though she were no longer sure she believed it herself. "I *have*."

"But now you've gone over the line. You've been getting more masculine every year, every day, sitting in this office, living a man's life, thinking like a man, acting like a man, accepting the responsibilities of a man. And now you've gone over for good."

He had to keep pacing, back and forth, nervously dragging on the cigarette. And he had to keep talking. He was wound up tighter than a drum. "You've gone over the line," he told her. "But Anita hasn't. And she isn't going to. You hear me? Because you're going to tell her—today, right now—that it's all over between you two, that she has to move out today. You're going to do this because you know now you can't lie to me any more, and you can't lie to anybody else, and even Jake will be able to see it in you now. So you're going to tell Anita it's all over. The two of you are finished."

"No." She sat up, slowly, as though it were painful to do so, and glared at him defiantly. "I won't give her up. I don't care what you do, I don't care who you tell, I'm not going to give her up."

"You are." He'd won this far, and he was going to win all the way. She wouldn't slip away from him now. "Because you don't want me to come in here again. You don't want me to test you again."

"I don't care what you do," she repeated, but her voice was shaking, and the fear was still bright in her eyes.

"You'll care," he said. He advanced on her, but a sudden shocked gasp to his left made him turn.

Anita was standing in the doorway between her office and Lavinia's, the back of one hand pressed to her mouth, staring at them. For a long second the three of them were frozen in tableau, and Barry knew that Anita could see what had happened in this office, but that she couldn't understand how or why it had happened.

"Anita!" They both cried the name at the same instant, and Barry took a step toward her, his hands out in supplication, while Lavinia twisted around and struggled to her feet.

At their movement Anita started to back away. Then she suddenly turned and fled across her own office to the hall door.

Barry cried, "Anita!" and started after her, but Lavinia lunged at him, knocking him aside, and ran through the doorway into Anita's empty office.

Barry ran after her, shouting, "Stay away from her!" He caught her at the other door and pulled her back from the doorway, hurling her across the room.

She came at him again, fingers curled into claws, trying to fight past him and out the door. They struggled, beating and pushing at one another, until finally he got a grip on her arm and bent her backward, tripping her and toppling her to the floor.

He stood over her, hunched, fully prepared to kill her if she tried to get up again. "You'll stay away from her," he panted, "or I'll kill you."

Lavinia suddenly crumpled, and rolled away onto her stomach, her hands pressed to her face, her shoulders shaking with racking sobs. "You've stolen her!" she whimpered. "I love her and you've stolen her away!"

He knew she was defeated for the moment, and so he ran from the office, past the startled Mrs. Marshall and down the hall to the elevators. But Anita was gone, and the arrow indicator above one of the doors showed the elevator was descending slowly to the main floor.

He jabbed the down button, ignoring the curious looks of the stenos. He paced back and forth in front of the elevator doors, cursing the slowness of the elevator, cursing the delay. By the time he got downstairs, she'd be out of the building.

Where would she go? He stopped his pacing, realizing that he had no idea where Anita would go from here. Not back to Lavinia's place, certainly, at least not yet. Where else?

The arrow indicator reached "1," and started back up, but there was no longer any need to hurry. By now, she was out of the building. And he had no idea at all where she would be heading for. She probably didn't have any idea herself.

He turned away from the elevators, passed through the wide-eyed glances of the stenos, and walked heavily down the long hall to his own office. On the way in, he said to

Miss Enright, "Tell Jake I'll be late with my copy again. Tell him I'll have it Monday for sure."

"Yes, Mr. Sanderson," she said, calm and efficient and passing no judgment on Mr. Sanderson's habitual laziness.

He went on into the office and sat down at his desk. "Well, Barry boy," he said to himself bitterly, "you sure fouled that up fine."

8

ANITA SAT on the studio couch in the apartment on West Forty-sixth Street, staring bleakly at the opposite wall and trying to decide what to do. She'd gone straight to Lavinia's apartment from the office, packed her things, and come here. The apartment was still empty, the roommate still out of town and no new girl had taken Anita's place.

Now it was seven o'clock in the evening, and she had been sitting here, unmoving, for almost three hours, staring at the opposite wall and trying to decide what to do.

She hadn't unpacked. Her suitcase still stood by the door. She'd thought of running away, of taking a train somewhere, of leaving New York completely. But there wasn't anywhere to go. Her parents were still in Europe, and the house was all closed up. And she couldn't go stay with any of her relatives, most of whom lived in New England. She would have to explain why she was there, and there was no explanation she could give.

The scene in Lavinia's office was etched in acid on her mind. Lavinia on the floor, half-naked, her skirt up around her waist, and Barry standing over her. It was so obvious what had happened in there. The whole room reeked of it.

And to think that she had been on the verge of going to Barry! After that impassioned speech he'd made, she'd done an awful lot of thinking. She'd almost gone over to his office to tell him that she wasn't going to stay with Lavinia after all.

There had been so many reasons for going to him. He had talked as though he wanted to marry her, or at least as though marriage was a possibility. And this thing with Lavinia could never be permanent anyway. She would eventually have to settle down, get married and have children and live a respectable life. She couldn't hide and be secretive and ashamed all of her life.

So she had almost gone to Barry. And then, when she was just on the verge of it, she had seen the two of them, the two people who claimed they wanted her, that they loved her and needed her—and it had been so very, very obvious what they had been doing together.

She couldn't go back to Lavinia now, not after that. She couldn't go to either of them, knowing what they had done together. Lavinia's lips would always bear the reminder of Barry, and Barry's lips would always bear the reminder of Lavinia. She could never stand to be near either of them again.

Yet, perversely, she still wanted them both. She wanted the comfort of Lavinia and she wanted the protection of Barry. She didn't know what she was going to do about it. She'd even thought of ending her life, of opening the window and just jumping out and solving everything forever.

She sat in the gathering darkness, miserable and lonely and frightened, and stared at the opposite wall, and wondered what was going to happen to her next.

She jumped at the sudden sound of the doorbell. It took her a moment to place what the sound meant. It came again, long and insistent, and without thinking, she ran across the room and pressed the buzzer. An instant too late she realized it must be either Barry or Lavinia, since no one else would be coming here. Now she had let them know she was in, and she would have to face them.

All right then, she would face them. She would get it over with once and for all, and be free of them forever.

She moved quickly around the room, turning on all the lights. Then the upstairs bell rang, and she tensed herself and opened the door.

It was Lavinia, looking haggard and drawn, looking older than Anita had ever seen her. "May I come in?" she asked, and the humility of her tone shocked Anita.

"Yes," she said, shaken by this change in Lavinia. She stepped aside to let the woman into the apartment.

Lavinia sat down on the studio couch, and her whole body seemed to sag. She looked fifty or older. The assurance and control that Anita had so much respected and depended upon had been swept away.

"You packed your things," Lavinia said. "I went home and all your things were gone." Her voice was flat and toneless, without life.

"Yes," said Anita. She felt a sudden overpowering urge to go to this woman, to hold her and comfort her and tell her that everything would be all right. But she fought the impulse, remembering the scene in Lavinia's office this afternoon, remembering the emotional state she had been in almost constantly since the first time she had gone to bed with Lavinia.

"I want to tell you what happened today," Lavinia told her.

"Lavinia, you don't have to——"

"I want to. Barry came to me and told me—ordered me—to give you up. He said you'd told him about us, and that you had gone to bed with him. He said he wanted you for himself."

"Lavinia, I was so upset, I had to talk to somebody——"

The older woman looked up at her with hurt eyes. "Couldn't you have talked to me? Did you have to tell Barry about us? Didn't you know he would only *use* it against us?"

Anita was silent, unable to answer. There were three Lavinias, and Anita could find no common denominator for them. There was the strong and loving Lavinia, at home in their apartment together. There was the lewd and obscene Lavinia, sprawled upon the office floor this afternoon. And there was this new, humble, hurt Lavinia. Anita was no longer sure which was the true Lavinia, or what Lavinia she could possibly love.

"I was afraid," Lavinia said. "I told Barry it was a lie, about me being—what he said. He said I'd have to prove it, and that there was only one way it could be proved. I was so afraid of the story getting out, I let him force me down onto the floor. I won't say he raped me because I didn't try very hard to stop him. I was too afraid. I wanted somehow to convince him that I wasn't—what he said." She looked up again, pleadingly. "Do you see, Anita? I *had* to do it. I hated it. I couldn't stand it, but I had to do it. Because you'd told him about us."

"Lavinia, I'm sorry," said Anita, meaning it sincerely, pitying the older woman and accepting her own blame. "I didn't know he'd do such a thing, I'm so terribly sorry."

"Come home with me," Lavinia said. "Please, Anita, come home with me. We can forget what happened today—"

"I can't," said Anita, and felt that tearing nervousness building within her again. "I can't live with you any more."

"We can forget this, Anita. Don't let it tear us apart."

"It isn't that." Anita moved nervously about the room, trying herself to understand what it was, what was wrong here, so that she could explain it to Lavinia. "It's the whole thing, it's—what we do together. It isn't right, no matter what. It can't last. We can't stay together forever. And I get so nervous and upset. That's why I had to talk to Barry—I was too nervous to eat or sleep or anything."

"You can always talk with me, Anita, you know that. And the nervousness will go away. I'll help you. We'll be able to help each other."

"I just can't *do* it." She was trying so hard to explain, without fully understanding herself what the problems were, and she knew she wasn't doing a good job of it. "I can't live that way, Lavinia, don't you see? That isn't the kind of life I want to lead. I'm just not that type of person. Someday I'll want to get married, have children—"

"Later, Anita. You have years yet. Can't you give me just a little time, just a little of yourself? Anita, I need you so much."

Anita stared helplessly out the window at the backs of buildings, empty clotheslines, and the concrete yard far below, and she thought again how simple it would be to open the window, to lean out, as though looking for something, to lean too far, to fall free, to sail and sail—

"Anita, come sit by me."

She turned away from the window, suddenly afraid of the direction of her thoughts. Lavinia was looking at her with open pleading. She couldn't stand to hurt people. She had never been able to stand hurting anybody.

"I wish I could explain," she said miserably. "I wish I could make you understand."

"Sit by me, please."

"All right." She came across the room and sat down beside Lavinia, but carefully not touching her. "Please don't touch me or try to kiss me or anything," she said.

"Anita, please. Look at me. I need you, Anita. I love you and I need you. Do you see I'm telling you the truth?"

Anita nodded, slowly. "I know you're telling the truth, Lavinia, and that's what makes it so difficult."

"Don't you want me at all any more?" Lavinia asked her. "You always liked me to hold you and kiss you."

How could she answer that? Anita's desire for Lavinia had always been so dependent upon the older woman's strength and self-sufficiency. Anita was the one who was weak and unsure, Lavinia the strong one. Anita had felt desire for that strong Lavinia, but she could feel no desire at all for this new, weak Lavinia. All she could feel for this Lavinia was pity.

But pity kept her from telling Lavinia the truth. Pity forced her to move closer to the other woman and let her touch her after all. Pity made her say, "I still like that, Lavinia. But I just can't live that way, don't you see?"

"Come close, baby," Lavinia murmured. "You look so troubled. We're both so troubled. We've had such a terrible, terrible day. We need each other, Anita."

Somehow it was happening again. Somehow she was letting Lavinia put her arms around her. Somehow she was turning up her face for Lavinia's kiss. Lavinia's hand was gentle on her breast, and despairingly she knew that it could start all over again. She knew that it would end the same way, with nervousness and emotional upset and confusion and misery, but that still it would start again here and now. Already they were lying back together on the studio couch, and Lavinia's lips were warm and soft on her own, and Lavinia's hands were stroking her yielding body.

She was touching Lavinia's breast and responding to Lavinia's kiss, when the upstairs doorbell sounded, and they broke apart like guilty schoolgirls.

Lavinia clutched her arm, pure panic on her face. "Don't answer!" she hissed. "It's Barry. Don't let him know we're here."

"But it's somebody right outside this door here," she objected. "How could he get in downstairs?"

"He'd ring somebody else's doorbell because he'd figure you wouldn't answer. Don't go near the door. He'll hear you!"

"We can't hide from him, Lavinia," she said, and with a sinking feeling knew that this was the mark of their love and that it could never be otherwise. Hiding and afraid, nervous and upset, shaken, trembling at the sound of a doorbell.

And this was what she had just been letting herself return to. She got up from the studio couch as the doorbell sounded again.

"Don't let him in," Lavinia whispered, harsh and frantic.

"We can't hide forever," she said. "We'll have to face him sometime." And she knew, all at once, that finally she was the strong one, that she was stronger than Lavinia, and the realization thrilled her. Yet at the same time it saddened her. To have no one strong to rely on, to have to be the strong one herself was sad and frightening.

She crossed the room, before this new strength should fail her, and pulled open the door.

Barry looked beyond her at Lavinia. "I want to talk to you, Anita," he said. "Alone." He seemed belligerent and angry, the way he had acted this afternoon when he had come to apologize to her. But now she understood that the belligerence was only the mask he wore when he was uncertain and confused. Now she felt stronger than he, too, and she wondered at this sudden well of strength in herself, and why it had taken such an emotional crisis to bring it to the surface.

"You can't talk to Anita alone," Lavinia was saying. Snarling, rather, like a vicious cat. "You can't talk to her at all. She wants nothing to do with you."

Barry grimaced and looked away from Lavinia to Anita. "I don't know what she's been telling you," he said, "but I want you to know the truth about this afternoon. It was her idea. She was going to prove to me she wasn't a lesbian. She taunted me into—"

"That's a lie!" Lavinia was standing now, glaring at Barry. "Don't listen to him, Anita, he's lying. He's trying to take you away from me. Don't listen to him."

"It doesn't matter what happened this afternoon, Barry," she said. "It doesn't matter which of you started it."

He came far enough into the room for her to be able to close the door, and said, "Anita, listen to me."

"I'm listening to you," she said. She thought how fumbling and ineffectual he was, then suddenly remembered that he wasn't always fumbling and ineffectual, suddenly remembered herself in bed with him, and she felt herself growing warm with embarrassment and—something else.

"I love you," he said. "I want to marry you."

"She won't have you," snapped Lavinia.

"I should have said this Monday night, but I didn't want to get involved. Now I *am* involved. I love you. I want you to come home with me and I want you to marry me."

"Anita," said Lavinia softly, "tell him that you're staying with me."

She looked from one to the other, knowing this was the moment, this was the final moment. She was going to have to make a decision that would affect her entire life.

Which of them did she want? With Lavinia, she could be a child forever. She could play that life was as simple as a pajama party. She need never grow up. Lavinia would comfort her, Lavinia would care for her. Lavinia would be strong again, when this was over. If she went back with Lavinia, Lavinia would once more be her strength and her protection.

But with Lavinia, she would have to hide all her life, she would have to live a lie forever. Did she want this? Was it worth it, to stay a child?

In Barry's arms, there were sensation and completeness that she would never find with Lavinia. In Barry's arms, she would be a woman.

"Tell him you love me," said Lavinia. "Tell him I'm the one you love."

Love? She didn't love either of them. She didn't love anybody yet, not in the way that Lavinia meant. They both claimed they loved her, yet how could she know whether they did or not, since she still didn't know what love was? She had to decide, here and now, but love couldn't help her.

Barry said he loved her. Barry wanted to marry her. To give her a husband, children, a home, everything she was supposed to want, supposed to have. With Barry, she would never have to hide.

She walked to him and took his hand. "I'll try to be good for you," she said.

Lavinia was there beside her, grabbing her arm, shrieking at her, her face twisted with rage. "You can't leave me, you swore you'd never leave me, you can't do it! Anita, you can't do this to me!"

"She's done it," said Barry, and Anita relaxed, because now he would be the strong one. She didn't have to be strong any more, she didn't have to try to explain, to understand.

"You get out of here!" Lavinia screamed at Barry, and lashed at his face with her fingernails. He ducked away, grabbing her arm, and said, "No, Lavinia, you've got it wrong. *You're* getting out." And he pulled her toward the door.

She twisted away from him, backing across the room. "I'll have your job, Barry. I'll have you thrown out of Chalmers-Mead in the morning."

He laughed at the threat, his arm now secure around Anita's waist. "There are plenty of jobs in this town, Lavinia," he said. "And I was getting more than a little sick of *Milady* anyway. So you can just take that housewives' Homer of yours and stow it—"

"Anita!" Lavinia was now glaring at her, and Anita flinched against Barry's chest, afraid the woman would attack her. "If you go with him—"

"She's going with me," Barry interrupted. "Don't bother firing her. She just quit. The same time I did. I'd love to hear you explain it all to Jake. Now, why don't you get out of here? There's nothing for you, Lavinia, nothing at all."

"I'm not leaving," she snapped. She looked farther away from them. "I'm not leaving until Anita comes to her senses. Anita, you know what kind of a man he is. You know what he did to me this afternoon."

"Bushwah," said Barry. He turned to Anita and motioned at the suitcases by the door. "Is this all your stuff?"

"Yes." She was afraid to look at Lavinia now. She'd never before seen a human being with so much hate and fury naked on her face.

"Since you won't leave," Barry told Lavinia, "we will. Make yourself right at home." He picked up the suitcases, and Anita opened the hall door. Barry said, "If you try to follow us, I'll slap you silly. That's a promise. You don't want to be a woman any more. All right, I won't treat you like a woman."

He stepped out into the hallway and waited for Anita to follow. She did, still avoiding Lavinia's eyes, and he slammed the door. "Come on," he said, and started down the stairs.

On the sidewalk, Barry flagged down a cruising cab. They stowed the suitcases into the trunk, and he gave the driver his address.

In the cab, she started to tremble uncontrollably. Lavinia's face, Lavinia's harshness . . .

Barry put his arm around her, and whispered, "All right, Anita, it's all right now. You won't ever have to see her again."

She huddled close to him, taking warmth and strength from him, and she knew she had made the right decision. And love—well, love would come in time. She would learn from him what love was.

She turned her face up to his and whispered his name. He kissed her, and Lavinia faded away.

9

WHEN BARRY AND ANITA WERE GONE, she could cry. She could fling herself down on the studio couch, beating it with tensed and straining fists, biting a pillow to hold down the screams of furious despair. When they were gone, she could release the tight grip of self-control, let the shattering waves of emotion pour over her and the burning tears flow free.

The fury of it died slowly, leaving Lavinia spent and exhausted, her body leaden, her eyes stinging, her lungs aching for air, her mind dulled by emotion. She lay on the couch, arms flung out and eyes closed, breathing shallowly and not trying to think.

She was alone. This was the first thought that clearly filtered through. She was now alone, more alone than she had ever been before in her life. There was no one, no one anywhere in the world who wanted her, who needed her, who could comfort her.

She thought fleetingly of Jake. He had always understood her. He had always known what to say to her, what to
do for her when she was blue or unhappy or surly. He had
loved her, and they had been fools not to marry, fools to
wait. Jake had loved her, and she clung to the thought.

But that had been eighteen years ago. Jake was now married—had been married for fourteen years, he had two children. Besides, he wasn't the same Jake. The Jake who had
loved her, the Jake she should have married, was long since
dead and buried.

Men, men, men . . . She thought of the men she had
known, remembering them one by one, their faces clear and
distinct in her mind, and she knew that Jake was the only
one of them who had truly loved her. And the only one
whom she had truly loved.

With sudden clarity, she saw them all, then saw herself
as she was today, and she knew that she could never go back
to any of them, because she too was someone else now. The
woman she had been was also dead and buried.

The encounter with Barry, this afternoon, came back to
her, and she shuddered at the memory of it, flinching not
from the brutal act itself, but from her own reaction to it.

When she was young—eighteen years ago, that other
Lavinia with that other Jake—love had been magnificent and
sex fantastically beautiful. But with the erosion of the years,
love had grown stale and sex had become perfunctory, the
pallid satisfaction of a bodily need scarcely more exciting
than the appeasement of hunger or thirst. So with the history
of years, as she had forced a place for herself in the world of
men, becoming a career woman to the exclusion of being
any other kind of woman, she had gradually become less and

less a woman, more and more a man, until now she was suspended, drained and empty, in that limbo between the sexes. She could never be more man than she was right now. And she could never return to being a woman.

This afternoon had proved that, once and for all. She had thought that she could fool Barry, that she could still be a woman in the arms of a man. But then he had come to her, and he had been anything but desirable. Instead he had been gross and obscene, a hulking monstrosity, more terrible than any creature in the dreams of frightened virgins.

Her greatest terror had been at this terror, the shattering discovery that she could no longer respond to a man, that her body instinctively shrank away from contact with a man, that somewhere in the last year she had crossed a line, and that she could no longer go back.

She had lived with that terror for hours now, and it hadn't lessened. She could no longer find love and companionship and fulfillment with a man, with any man. If the old Jake were alive today—perhaps not even with him.

She could not share herself with any man. And most women would turn away from her. She had cut herself off from almost all of the human race, and only the thought that she could still regain Anita had kept her from succumbing immediately to her despair.

Now Anita, too, was gone. Gone forever, the one last person she had to turn to. And she was alone.

She couldn't stand to be alone. She had to find someone, anyone, to protect her from the aching silence of being alone.

This apartment she was in was so small, so close, so empty. All at once, she couldn't bear to stay in this room any longer. She got to her feet, pulled on her coat, and fled from the apartment down the stairs to the street.

She stopped on the sidewalk. Where now? There was nowhere for her to go. Only her own apartment—and how much emptier that would be without Anita, the emptiest place in the world, the loneliest place in creation.

She started walking, aimlessly, toward Times Square. It was almost eight o'clock in the evening, and the sidewalk, east of Eighth Avenue, was crowded with people, emerging from the restaurants that lined that block of Forty-sixth Street and strolling toward the theaters. Playgoers, smiling, chatting, walking two by two. There were couples and quartets, and Lavinia, moving among them, felt she was the only one who was alone.

At Times Square, she turned south, but the crowds here were even heavier, and always she was the only one alone. There had to be somewhere she could go, people she could be with, people of her own kind—

People of her own kind. She remembered, all at once, a bar she had gone to with Sandra, near Sheridan Square down in the Village, a hangout for people like her. "People like me," she whispered, accepting it, and a dark melancholy flowed through her.

She stepped to the curb, out of the crowd, and waved at a cruising cab. She climbed into the back seat, said, "Sheridan Square," and fixed her gaze resolutely on the meter and the licenses attached to the dashboard, not looking out at the crowds that moved along Seventh Avenue, two by two.

At Sheridan Square, the driver said, "Anyplace in particular?"

"No," she said, wondering why she didn't want the cab driver, whom she would never see again, to know where it was she was going. "No, right here is all right."

She paid him and got out, looking around to get her bearings. Side streets came into the square from all directions, Grove, Christopher, Bleecker, West Fourth—it took her a minute or two to decide where the bar would be. Sandra had lived down to the right on Grove Street, and they had come from that direction, crossing Seventh Avenue and going up this way toward Gay Street.

She started off, took one wrong turn amid the twisted jumble of tiny Village streets, and finally found the place. It was in the basement of an old building, and a steep flight of concrete steps led down to the front door. The original windows had been bricked up, and the wall painted with whitewash. An amateurishly drawn name was scrawled on the whitewashed brick above the door: "Al's." There was no neon sign, no further indication that behind this blind wall was hidden a bar. The door was wood and windowless, and also painted white. The whitewash had been applied to both bricks and door years ago, and was now a dull and dirty gray.

She went down the steps and pushed open the door. A wave of heat and noise poured out at her, with the acrid smell of a poorly ventilated bar. She went on inside, and stood for a second, until her eyes had grown accustomed to the orange-neon gloom of the interior.

The place was jammed. Boys who were not entirely boys, and girls who were not entirely girls, stood three deep at the long bar on the right, and more of them were packed into the dim booths to the left and at the back of the long room. The women were mostly dressed in slacks and shirts and jackets, and few of them wore make-up of any kind. Most of them had relatively short hair, combed straight back from their scrubbed-clean foreheads. The men, on the other hand, were garishly dressed, with loud shirts and tight black trousers—red or silver stripes ran down the seams of some of these trousers—and many of them had on rouge and eye make-up and even lipstick, while most of them wore their hair longer than the women, carefully waved and coiffured.

A tiny, mincing boy squirmed in front of Lavinia, his hands clasped across his chest, his eyes wide with affected pleasure. "Why, *Mary!*" he shrieked. "You're in drag tonight, dearie, and you look *stunning!* Oh, do come back to *my* booth. I want to get to know you *better!*"

Lavinia frowned at him with disgust. "I *am* a woman," she said. "I don't think you'd be interested."

His look of shock was as affected and overdone as had been his look of pleasure. "Oh! I *thought* you were too good to be true!" And he hopped away again.

A woman at the bar, just to Lavinia's right, turned at the exchange and studied Lavinia slowly and carefully. Finally she said, "Are you sure you're in the right place, Madam?"

Lavinia coldly returned her look. "What do you think?"

The woman calmly continued her study, then raised her eyebrows, smiled a bit, and said, "In that case, let me buy you a drink."

"Please do," said Lavinia. The noise and ostentatious show of this place were unnerving.

"You're drinking—?"

Lavinia moved closer, to see what the woman herself was drinking. Beer. Most of the women were drinking beer, most of the men drinking complicated mixed drinks, ones calling for grenadine and crème de cacao and sugar and lemon peel. "I'll have a beer," she said, though she really wanted something stronger.

"You don't sound happy about it," said the woman. "You want a shot with it?"

Lavinia nodded. "Yes. Thanks."

The bartender was female, her huge, broad-shouldered, heavy-bosomed bulk encased in a dirty white apron, her short black hair plastered to her scalp with perspiration. Lavinia's new friend called to her, "Al! Two more down this way."

"In a minute, in a goddamn minute."

The woman pushed the boy next to her, making room for Lavinia at the bar. He glowered at her, but didn't say anything, and went back to his animated conversation with another boy.

"I'm Harry Martin," said the woman conversationally, and she said the name so naturally that Lavinia understood that, whatever her name had originally been, she now thought of herself exclusively as Harry Martin.

"I'm—Vincent Cartwright."

"What do they call you? Vinnie? I will, anyway. How are you, Vinnie?" And she thrust out her hand for Lavinia to shake.

Lavinia shook the hand, and then the name struck off its echo. She had chosen Vincent because it was the first male name that came to her that was close enough to her own name, so that she would be able to remember it readily. It hadn't occurred to her that it would be shortened to Vinnie.

Jake had called her Vinnie. No one else in all her life had called her Vinnie, except Jake, long long ago.

She fought away from that echo, concentrated on this woman who called herself Harry Martin. She was of medium height, and just a bit on the chunky side. She was wearing mannish shoes, tan slacks, a man's white shirt open at the collar and a tan corduroy jacket, like a basketball jacket, with snaps down the front. Her face was scrubbed clean, without make-up, and her hands were bare of rings or nail polish. Her hair was mouse-brown, short, and brushed straight back above a squarish plain face with level eyes and a broad, thin-lipped mouth. She stood the way a man would stand, one foot up on the bar rail, one elbow on the bar, her shoulders hunched slightly, her head thrust slightly forward.

"Let me make a couple of guesses about you," said the woman. (It was impossible for Lavinia to think of her as Harry, and there was no other name to put in its place.) "From the look of you, I'd say you were either a new recruit or you're passing for straight on the outside. Probably both."

Lavinia nodded. "You're right. Both."

"And this is your first time in here, right?"

"No. My second time."

"Okay. I'll keep on guessing. You're on the rebound from your first girl-girl romance. Am I right? She brought you here once, so naturally you came back when you found yourself all alone again. Right?"

"Close enough," said Lavinia. "It's more complicated than that."

"It's always more complicated than that, Vinnie," said the woman matter-of-factly. "Take it from me. I don't come to this place often. It gets on my nerves. To tell you what I'm doing here tonight would take hours. It's always complicated."

"You're on the rebound, too," said Lavinia.

The woman nodded. "And it can always be simplified," she said. "You're right, I'm on the rebound, too. Only it isn't my first." She laughed. "Far from my first, Vinnie boy, far from it."

Their drinks came then, and Harry raised the shot glass of bar whiskey and drank it in one gulp, then reached for the beer. Lavinia followed her example, and the whiskey was already in her stomach before she felt it burn at the back of her throat. A quick swallow of beer cut the burning to a pleasant tingle.

A sudden cacophony of shrieks erupted from the booths at the back, and a high-pitched, not-quite-male voice began to scream something unintelligible about being two-timed. Al, the heavy-set bartender, waded through the crowded customers, her face grim, and the shrieking stopped as suddenly as it had begun.

Harry emptied her beer glass and said, "In another half-hour, there'll be a riot in here. And then the law. It's getting near the end of the month, and too dangerous to be attracting the police."

"Why's that?"

"They've got a monthly arrest quota. They've got to keep the number of arrests high, so they'll have good statistics to wave at anybody who says they're goofing off. Toward the end of the month, they start raiding places like this, so they can make the arrest quota." She shrugged. "It doesn't mean much, just a night in jail and a suspended sentence the next morning. But then you're down on the books, and they're liable to come around and pick you up every month, when they're pushing to make the quota. So far I've managed to keep away from the law, and I'd like to maintain the record. Maybe we ought to get out of here."

The idea of being arrested as a homosexual terrified Lavinia. The story would get around. It would have to for she was too important in her field. "I think we should," she agreed.

Harry grinned at her. "Don't look so scared. They won't be coming around for half an hour yet anyway, maybe longer. You've got plenty of time to finish your beer."

Nevertheless, Lavinia gulped the beer as rapidly as she could, and the two of them left the bar and went up the steps to the street.

"*You're* all right out here," Harry told her. "You look straight. But I'm afraid a cop would see me coming from a mile off." She grinned crookedly. "I'm not camouflaged very well. So I'd rather not spend too much time on the sidewalk."

Lavinia looked around, but the street was dark and nearly deserted, with only a few cellar bars and the dark hulks of the buildings. "Where then?" she asked.

"None of the places like Al's," said Harry. "They'll all be too dangerous tonight. Look, I live over on Christopher Street, just across the square. Why don't we buy a six-pack and go on over there?"

Lavinia looked at this woman. She was more obviously and definitely homosexual than anyone Lavinia had ever known before. But didn't that merely mean that she was just more honest than someone like, say, Sandra? Or Lavinia herself? And she was a person, a human being, someone to be with and to help push back the encroaching darkness of solitude.

"That sounds like a good idea," she said.

"Come on, then." Harry linked her arm with Lavinia's, and they walked back toward Sheridan Square.

At Seventh Avenue, between Grove and Christopher streets, there were a grocery store and a liquor store side by side. While Harry went to the grocery store for the beer, Lavinia stopped in the liquor store for a bottle of whiskey. Then they walked up Christopher Street to Harry's place, a three-room apartment on the fourth floor of an ancient and ramshackle building near the other end of the block.

"This is a pretty big place for one person," Harry said, as they walked into the apartment. "I had a roommate up until a couple of days ago, but we had a fight and she moved out. Take off your coat. I'll stow this beer away in the refrigerator."

Lavinia took off her coat and sat down on the sagging sofa. The apartment was scrupulously clean but seedy. It had obviously come furnished, with the worn and faded furniture inevitable in such apartments, and Harry had added practically nothing of her own. A small bookcase near the sofa was filled with paperbound books on philosophy, government and Greek mythology. A Japanese water color hung on the wall above the bookcase, an outdoor scene in summer, with fragile and drooping trees geometrically placed on a green and gradual slope.

Harry came back with two cans of beer and two water glasses containing an inch of whiskey apiece. She was balancing the water glasses on the beer cans, and said, "Rescue me, *s'il vous plait*."

Lavinia took the water glasses, and Harry sat down beside her on the sofa. "I hope you don't mind drinking the beer out of the can," she said. "These are all the glasses I have left." She smiled apologetically. "There were some, uh, violent arguments around here."

"I don't mind," said Lavinia.

Harry traded Lavinia one of the beer cans for one of the glasses, and leaned back to say, "Let's get the personal history over with right away. I'm Harry, as I told you. I'm a set designer and a good one. Two off-Broadway shows are playing in front of my sets right this minute. Unfortunately, set designing isn't steady money, so I also work as a secretary. To Jack Kingsley. I don't know if you've heard of him."

Lavinia shook her head. "I don't think so."

"He's also a set designer. The difference is, he's successful at it. More successful than me, I mean. He does Broadway work mostly, and some television. He's a screaming fag, but he tries to pass for straight, so he daren't have one of his boyfriends for a secretary. The theory is that I cover for him and he covers for me. We both try to imply that we're sleeping together." She grinned. "I don't think we've managed to fool anybody," she said, "but Jack is satisfied. And I get a steady income that way, so I'm satisfied, too."

She drank the whiskey at a gulp and sipped from the beer can. "I'm twenty-six years old," she went on. "I was born in Lincoln, Nebraska, and I've been in New York five years. End of personal history. How about you?"

"I'm a magazine editor," Lavinia told her, trying to decide how much to tell about herself. "I'm forty years old, I've lived in New York most of my life, and I really don't want to talk about the past."

"I know what you mean," said Harry, smiling again. She drank more beer, put the can and the empty glass on the table beside her, and said, "I'm glad we ran into each other tonight. You'll never know how lonely I've been the last few days."

"Oh, yes, I will," Lavinia told her. "I know all about being lonely."

"We don't have to be lonely any more," said Harry. "Come over here."

Lavinia put down the glass and beer can. This was the moment, the new beginning. She moved closer to Harry, and looked at the woman's face, and saw the face of a stranger.

I don't know you, she thought all at once. I don't know you so how can we come together so casually? There should be something more than this, more preparation. We should get to know each other, slowly and completely, get to know who we are and how well we blend together. It shouldn't be like this, like casual animals in a field at night.

Harry put her arm around her and drew her close, and her lips were cool on Lavinia's, her body chunky and hard, her hand rough and insistent. Lavinia recoiled from the touch, pushing the woman away and sitting back wide-eyed.

"What's the matter?" Harry was reaching for her again, looking annoyed. All at once she stopped, her hands poised in the air, and peered at Lavinia from narrowed eyes. "Are you sure you've been with a woman before? Are you sure this isn't the first time?"

Lavinia shook her head, trying to think, trying to get things in order in her mind. "It isn't the first time," she said. "There were two women—before. But it was different. It wasn't like this."

"Look, Vinnie, you came to me. I didn't come to you. You picked me up."

"I don't know." Lavinia turned away, not understanding what was wrong here, not understanding her own feelings, knowing only that she couldn't do things this way. She couldn't be such a casual and impersonal animal. "I was alone," she said, trying to explain to both of them. "I was lonely, and I wanted somebody—somebody to talk to, to get to know, to keep me from being lonely. But not like this— we don't know each other at all, we just met a few minutes ago."

"So what?" Harry reached out, grasping Lavinia's arm, twisting her around to face her. "Look at me, dammit," she snapped. "What difference does it make? You're butch and so am I. We're different from those people outside. Their laws and rules don't count with us. We don't have to wait to be properly introduced. We don't have to go through any long courtship and we don't have to play games with each other for weeks or months. You want sex, I want sex. It's as simple as that. We both want the same thing, and we both want it the same way. Why build a huge scene out of it?"

"I just—this isn't the way I expected it, that's all."

The girl was getting angry now. "Who the hell cares what you expected? You came down to Al's. You picked me up. You made an offer and you're going to stick to it."

Lavinia pulled out of the woman's grasp, getting to her feet. "I don't even know you," she cried. "You're a stranger—somebody I just met. How can we mean anything to each other? How could we do anything and have it mean anything at all?"

"I don't care about meanings," said Harry, rising from the sofa. "I'm not interested in any of that garbage. So what if we just met? Maybe this'll be a one-night stand. You'll stay here tonight and leave tomorrow and we'll never see each other again. Or maybe we'll get to like being together, and we'll stay together for a while, for a month or a year or however long. What difference does it make? That's the way our life is, that's all. What the hell do you want me to do—marry you before I can get into bed with you?"

"We've got to know each other first." Lavinia gestured helplessly, frightened by the girl's belligerence, trying to explain so she would understand. "We've got to at least talk to each other, get to know each other."

"I know all I need to know." She advanced on Lavinia, her mouth set in a grim line. "You picked me up. You made me an offer. Now you're going to deliver."

Lavinia tried to back away, but Harry gripped her wrist, yanking her close, and slowly forced her around toward the sofa again. Lavinia struggled to free herself, and Harry slapped her ringingly across the face. "You're not backing out, you lily-white bitch," she snarled. "You're going to deliver."

"Let me alone!" Lavinia managed to twist away once more, and ran across the room toward the door. But Harry got there first, spun her around and hit her, twice, in the stomach and the breast, punching with closed fists like a man.

The punch in the stomach knocked the breath out of Lavinia, and the blow to her breast sent jagged, piercing streaks of pain knifing through her body. She screamed and fell back against the door, holding her breast.

Harry slapped her open-handed across the face once more, and said, "If I have to kick the crap out of you, Vinnie, I'll do it. Are you going to cut out this foolishness and be nice to me or aren't you?"

"Please," gasped Lavinia, blinking away the tears. Her breast burned with pain, making her weak and nauseous. She sagged, sliding down against the door to her knees, and huddled there in abject fear. "Please," she whispered again. "Don't, please. I'm sorry, but I can't. Not this way. Don't force me, please."

"Goddamn you!" screamed the girl, standing over her. "Do you think you can back out now? I could have found anybody in that place—anybody who was there, and there wouldn't have been any of this crap. But *you picked me up*. Do you think I dare go outside again tonight? The police will be prowling this section so tight by now I wouldn't get ten feet from the front door. Do you think I can get myself somebody else?"

"I'm sorry," whispered Lavinia. "I thought I could—I didn't know it would be like this. I'm sorry, truly sorry. If you'll only let me go—"

"And what about *me*?" Harry was shrieking at her now, her face red with rage, a vein standing out blue and swollen in her throat, her hands balled into fists at her sides. "What am *I* supposed to do?"

Lavinia shook her head helplessly. There was nothing more she could say.

Harry glared down at her for a moment longer, then suddenly exhaled explosively and turned away. "The hell with you," she muttered. "I wouldn't get anything out of it if I had to force you. Go on, get out of here."

Lavinia looked up, not believing the reprieve. Harry stood on the other side of the room, facing away from her. It was true. She was free to go.

She struggled to her feet, still trembling, her breast still aching, but less fiercely now, and got her coat from the chair where she had tossed it. "Thank you," she said gratefully. "I'm sorry, I—"

"Don't talk to me. Just get out of here."

Lavinia hesitated, understanding what the girl had meant, why she was so angry, but unable to accept the shallow and meaningless code the girl lived by. But anything she could say would only serve to make the girl angrier still. She left the apartment, closing the door carefully behind her, and when she was halfway down the first flight of stairs, she heard the sound of a flung glass smashing against the wall.

She hurried the rest of the way to the street and stood for a moment on the pavement, inhaling the cold night air, giving herself time to grow calm, to recover.

Time to realize that she had solved nothing, that she was still alone, that there was still no place for her to go. Further, even a woman she had thought of as her own kind had failed her. There was nothing left.

Why couldn't she have gone along with the woman? What difference would it have made?

She didn't know. All she knew was that she couldn't do things that way, that she wasn't interested solely in sex. She was interested in companionship, in the end of loneliness, in someone with whom to share herself.

If the girl had only gone more slowly, if she had only mimicked interest in Lavinia as a person for a while, instead of immediately turning to sex, as though there was nothing else in the world that they could share.

If only she had married Jake . . .

She started to walk, directionless, purposeless. When she got back to Seventh Avenue and the square, she stopped again. The subway entrance was to her right, cruising cabs flowed by, diners and restaurants and bars were bright-lit and inviting. Yet there was no place for her to go.

She walked again, looking at the people she passed on the street, looking through the windows of a diner at the people sitting at the counter, wondering what she was going to do, where she was going to go, how she was going to live from now on.

Without thinking about it, without paying any attention to the direction her feet were taking, she turned onto Grove Street, and walked slowly along. She stopped when she realized she was in front of the building where Sandra had lived when Lavinia first met her. And she had heard that Sandra had moved back into the same apartment.

Lavinia remembered the first months of their relationship, and how fine they had seemed. How fine they had *been*.

She knew Sandra so much better now. She knew the girl's viciousness and pettiness, she knew her self-centeredness.

Knowing these things, knowing Sandra as well as she now did, could they begin again? They could build so much more stable a relationship now, knowing each other so well.

Stop fooling yourself, Lavinia, she told herself angrily. Sandra knows you as a person, that's all that matters. Sandra will pretend to love you and to care what happens to you. And that's the best you can expect now.

But it's better than nothing.

The decision was made before she knew it, and she was running up the front steps, wondering if Sandra was home, praying that Sandra would be home. She pressed the down-stairs bell, and after an eternity the buzzer sounded, and Sandra was home.

It was four flights up, with no elevator, and she started at a run, but at the second flight she forced herself to stop. She couldn't go to Sandra this way, running, overeager, ob-viously, begging. She cast about for a story, for some way to meet Sandra as an equal, and could find none.

Well, it didn't matter that she had no story. Nothing mattered but that she wouldn't be alone. She climbed the rest of the way to the fourth floor. Sandra was waiting in the doorway.

"Hello," said Lavinia.

Sandra nodded, curt and suspicious.

"May I come in?"

"If you want."

Sandra stepped to one side, and Lavinia walked into the apartment. Sandra motioned for her to sit down, and took a seat across the room from her, waiting for her to begin.

"I want you back, Sandra," said Lavinia. There was no better way to say it. The only thing to do was to tell it the way it was, and get it over with.

Sandra looked surprised for a moment, and then she smiled. "Anita walked out on you, is that it?"

"Yes. She's marrying Barry Sanderson. Sandra, listen. I don't have any illusions about you, and I don't think you have any about me. I want you back, but I don't want you working at *Milady* again. You have a career. We'll get along much better if we leave it at that."

"That's the condition?"

"Yes. The only one."

Sandra nodded. "I would have one or two conditions of my own, you know."

"Yes, I suppose so."

"I would have the right to go where I wanted, when I wanted, and with whom I wanted, and without having either to account to you or lie to you."

Lavinia closed her eyes. But to share someone with others was still better than to have no one to share. She nodded.

"Then I'd like to come back, Lavinia. We didn't get along very well before, but I think that was because we didn't have any solid agreement. I think we could get along better now."

"I hope so," said Lavinia.

Sandra studied her, frowning, and finally asked. "Why *did* you come back to me, Lavinia?"

"I was lonely, Sandra. I was terribly lonely."

"Everyone is lonely," Sandra said coldly. She got to her feet. "Everyone is locked alone inside his own head."

"I know."

"Don't think you've got a patent on loneliness, Lavinia. I've been lonely, too. And we'll be lonely again. That's the way things are with people like us and there's not much we can do about it."

The End

About the Author

Edwin West is the pen name of a popular writer who has written many short stories and who has two hardcover novels to his credit, both published by Random House. He has lived most of his life in New York City and during the warmer months spends part of his time away from his typewriter playing bit parts in summer stock with his wife, who is an accomplished actress.

Also on Blackbird . . .

ELIZABETH TAYLOR

by

John B. Allan

⌘

THE CASE OF JENNIE BRICE

by

Mary Roberts Rinehart

⌘

Hart Island

a novel by

Seth Edgarde

BLACKBIRD BOOKS
www.bbirdbooks.com